GAME OVER

by

ELLIOT TORRES

First Edition
Printed in USA

ISBN: 978-1-7373411-0-9 (paperback)
ISBN: 978-1-7373411-1-6 (ebook)

Facebook: @MrElliotTorres
Instagram: @MrElliotTorres
Twitter: @MrElliotTorres
Website: elliottorres.com

Cover Design by Rafael Andres
Author Photo by chriscarlislephotography.com

PRESENT DAY

HOLLYWOOD HILLS
LOS ANGELES, CALIFORNIA

I reach for my one-liter alkaline bottled water. Anything else would be unacceptable. Shielded by my black-rimmed, Tom Ford aviator sunglasses, the rest of my toned, fit body is at the sun's mercy. Naturally tanned, thanks to my Puerto Rican parents, I have a love affair with the sun. The only thing that gets between us is SPF 30 because I am not interested in aging prematurely. For anyone else, this would be a two-week vacation once a year or weekends by the pool. However, this is my life. There is no such thing as nine-to-five because this is twenty-four-seven. I won't be retiring at the age of sixty-seven, because I already have. This is thirty. I beckon my housekeeper. "Lupita, ven aquí por favor." "Okay mijo." She walks over from the living room through the sliding glass doors and onto the pool area overlooking Los Angeles. "¿Qué necesitas?" "Toallas por favor." "Okay, no problema," she said. She retreats into my contemporary home as I continue to rest and recover from my bruises and wounds while I try to find a comfortable angle as I bask in the sun.

Although I try to meditate my thoughts away, I can't help but to keep thinking of the pain I had to endure to get to this moment. However, the point is, I am here. For some, being underestimated is infuriating, but for me, I use it as fuel. The most dangerous people aren't those you can easily recognize as a threat, it's those who blend in. Lupita returns with the white towels and places them on the lounge table. She walks back into my house and returns to mopping the floors. I like everything meticulous and minimal. My stark white home radiates zen simplicity. I turn to look at Lupita as she rings out the mop in the bucket of crimson filled water. It's not the shade of a powerful disinfectant but instead the color of death. She casually continues to mop the blood off the floor. I turn my head, close my eyes, and peacefully fall asleep. This is the life I dreamed of.

CHAPTER 1

FIVE YEARS EARLIER

"Inmate 2569153013, Michael Chapman, today is your release date. Your day has finally come," the warden said. A muscular, Caucasian man with a shaved head stands up and approaches the cell door. It had been two years since Mike Chapman was arrested after a large amount of Cocaine and an unregistered gun was found in his Porsche when he was caught speeding on his way to Las Vegas. He could have gotten five years, but due to his connections and white privilege, he was able to get the sentencing down to two. He is Mike Chapman, a multi-millionaire and the mastermind behind the most violent video games that set the standard for what all of the gamers are playing today. He pushes boundaries, angers parents, and has a cult following. To the everyday Angeleno driving past him on the 405, he's just another asshole on the road, but to gamers, he is the god of gaming.

Mike is escorted through the cell block as the other inmates witness the departure of the notorious man they've come to respect. "Yo, Mike, don't forget about us." "Mike, kick ass out there!" "For sure." He gives the peace sign and emerges out of the correctional facility to a parked Mercedes SUV.

The driver, a tall, heavy set Middle Eastern man, with short-styled hair, beard and signature black leather jacket that could barely contain him emerges from the vehicle opening the back door for Mike. "Hi, Marek, good to see you man." "It's good to have you back, boss." "Cut the formal shit, we're family." Mike pats him on the back. Mike gets in the back of the SUV and is greeted by his sister Rachael Chapman. In an insincere, excited tone. "Welcome back big brother." "Cut the bullshit, you loved running my company while I was gone." "Everything has been going smoothly." "Well, the king is back so you can go back to doing what you were doing before, which is taking orders from me." "You're welcome asshole, I've kept Imperial on top while you've clearly been pumping iron." "Fuck, all there is to do in there is workout. Now, I can get back to the throne." "What's your first order of business? Your highness." "I want to create a game based on the '80s movie *Bad Boys*." "Oh, the one with Sean Penn." "Yes, but Sean before Madonna." "I like that, just another game to piss off the parents and stir up some controversy. It's what we do best." "It's what I do best. Cut this kumbaya democracy bullshit. The dictator is back." She looks out the window. "Yes, I know, the dick is back," she says under her breath. "Funny, don't forget who signs your checks. Even with me having been locked away you still have been getting paid. And that's because of me." "How could I forget? You remind me every day." Mike points to her. "I want to make sure you don't." "We're here boss," Marek said. Marek parks the SUV and walks around to open the door for Mike. "Fuck yeah. Game On."

CHAPTER 2

INSERT COIN

I had been working at the Los Angeles Public Library's Downtown branch for a month and a half, as a six-month temp while things were slow with my acting. I was trying to get my big break but, like every artist in Los Angeles, I had to pay the rent. I was surrounded by dusty books in the middle of a sweltering summer. I had to lug the books in an old walnut cart, which would fit about 100 of them at a time, double stacked. In between scanning them into the library's system, I would search the internet for castings to get me out of this monotonous job and into Hollywood, Bollywood, even porn would have worked as long as I made excellent money and became famous. I hoped it came sooner rather than later.

This was my life on Mondays, Wednesdays, and Fridays. I was also a bartender on Thursdays, Saturdays, and Sundays at The Back Door in West Hollywood. Monday mornings were always grueling for me as I attempted to recuperate from the weekend shift. I arrived at the annex, which housed other collections from the central branch. The only good thing about this location was that there weren't many of us in the enormous space. I walked up the stairs and into the elevator pressing the 2nd floor. I arrived at my job, or as the employees referred to it, "the dungeon." "Hi, Melissa, how are you?" "I am good, thanks, how was your weekend?" "Uneventful, I worked." "I hear you, now we are back in this shithole," she said as she rolled her eyes. "Tell me about it." "I did get a new tattoo, though," she said as she pulled her bright, red tank-top over her head to expose her back. She showed me a vibrant Japanese mask adorning her pale skin. "That's number eight, right?" "Yup, you have to hurry up and get your first one," she said as she winked. "By the way, have you heard back from your audition?" "No, not yet."

As I proceeded to my desk, I heard the footsteps of our over-enthusiastic boss. It sounded as though he was wearing stilettos, and I'm sure in his mind they were. Who the hell gets excited about inventorying books? I mean, who reads anymore? My boss was a tall, skinny effeminate gay man. His name was Garrett Thompson. He spoke with a variety of expressions mostly using his arms. I couldn't tell if he was swatting a fly or just being dramatic. He stressed the importance of meeting daily quotas with the number of books we scanned. "Good morning, team!" he shouted. Did I forget to mention he was always so damn chipper about this boring shit? I believed Garrett got hard-ons from his job. "Good morning," we all responded with groans under our breaths. "Okay, people, let's get through as many stacks as possible today." He scrolled down the tattered sheet of paper he was holding to tell us what sections of the annex we would be working in. "Here is the list of new editions that have to be inventoried. Latin America, Renaissance, Psychology, Social Sciences, and Nature." He looked up with a nauseating grin on his face. "Okay, let's get started," he shouted as he clapped. He retreated into his dark, fluorescent-lit office while we returned to work under unforgiving lighting and dust mite infested stacks.

We all moved sluggishly, wishing we could be anywhere else. Did I fail to mention there were no windows? Yes, that's right, no windows so we had to daydream looking at vanilla-colored walls with a dingy ceiling probably layered in asbestos while the rest of Angelenos were kissed by the sun. Okay, maybe I am being a little dramatic, but I am an actor after all. My routine was simple: get as many books on my cart as humanly possible so I could stay at my desk longer, search for castings, and submit my headshot along with my resume. I did this daily until 5:00 p.m. and figured at some point, a gig had to surface. I had been sending headshots to several casting agencies and open calls. I also sent the day job version of my resume to the many media empires that created some of my favorite programming and films. Sony, HBO, NBC, ABC, Netflix, Hulu, I mean everywhere. If they were producing films, television, or entertainment of any sort, I wanted to be a part of it in some capacity, even as an assistant. I figured working as an assistant behind the scenes would be a good way to meet someone who could get me closer to my goal. I definitely didn't move to Los Angeles to become a librarian. In college, I avoided assigned readings and used CliffsNotes instead. I had to read a book for one of my finals because the exam was based solely on the reading material. I blew it off because I was invited, by a former fling, to attend an industry party at the Chateau Marmont. I visited my professor's office to show my interest and effort in the subject. I knew I had failed the final; I blew my professor and managed to get a B in the class. I spent more time in the bars and nightclubs than I did in the classroom. The city educated me in other ways that usually led to a bedroom and originally being from Chicago, Los Angeles can be a distracting city to attend college.

After my first three months working at the library, on a Wednesday afternoon, I received a call but I didn't recognize the number. "Hello," I said. A woman on the other line began speaking. "Hi, can I speak to Joaquin Otero please?" "Speaking," I responded in a hopeful energetic tone. "Hi, this is Brenda Ramirez from Imperial Games." I was surprised and excited at the same time. "Oh, hi, how are you?" "I'm fine, thanks. I received your resume for the office assistant position and was wondering if you are available to come in for an interview?" I was trying to remember when I sent this resume because it wasn't exactly at the top of my list, but the company had some controversial press recently regarding their video games. They also hired actors and celebrities to do the voiceovers. It wasn't the silver screen, but it wasn't dusty books either. "Sure, I can come in." "Great, can you come in on Friday at 2:00 p.m.?" "Yes, that works for me." "Okay, I will email you the details and will see you then." She quickly hung up the phone. I placed my phone in my pocket and began going through a list of things I had to get done before the interview. I had to shave, make sure my jacket was interview ready, and print a few copies of my resumes. I grabbed a dozen more books and pushed my cart away. The day began to look brighter.

After college, I moved around to various areas in the city and landed in Hollywood on the West Hollywood border. It was gritty but my one-bedroom apartment had a lot of light coming in and I had a view of the Hollywood Hills, the Hollywood Sign and the Griffith Observatory. When I decided to rent the apartment, I knew it was right for me because I could keep my goal in plain sight. I visualized myself living in the Hollywood Hills someday but until then, I lived in a one-bedroom walk-up with my boyfriend, Vaughn. He was an aspiring actor as well. We were two hungry actors wanting the same thing and shared an insatiable appetite for sex. He'd been working as a waiter at Marix while I worked my two jobs.

When I walked into the apartment, I noticed something was different. V wasn't home and I froze. I stared at the sofa because he was usually sitting on it playing video games but instead there was pure silence. I walked into the bedroom and noticed that several things were missing. I quickly began opening our drawers and realized that many of his belongings were gone. I turned to the closet, opened the door, and his clothes were gone. In the mirror hanging on the door, I could see in the reflection a piece of paper with my name on it sitting on the dresser. I walked over to read it.

Dear Joaquin, I hate to do this in a letter, but I knew I wouldn't be able to face you. We've been having problems for a while now and I know that we both have been holding on, but I can't anymore. I've met someone and I love him. You and I tried our best but after three years, I can't try anymore. I don't want to. I realized that I went from being in love with you to no longer loving you. I don't want you to blame yourself, we just grew apart. It happens. I wish you all the happiness in the world. V.

I tore the letter up, grabbed the lamp on the nightstand and threw it against the mirror. The glass shattered just like my heart. I fell to my knees and began to cry with my face buried on the bed. I truly loved him and wanted things to work out, but I can't be with someone who doesn't want to be with me. I walked to my fridge and poured myself some Belvedere vodka and club soda followed by another. I cried myself to sleep that night.

CHAPTER 3

TGIF

In my mind, I tried to exude confidence, but I couldn't help but feel so empty inside. I needed to make sure that my sadness didn't show. I had to be strong on the outside despite the fact I was crumbling on the inside. I walked into a building not too far from my current job on a quiet industrial street in the arts district of Downtown Los Angeles. I hoped the interview wouldn't take long because I was worried about my car. We weren't too far from Skid Row and some of the streets resemble an episode of *The Walking Dead*. None of that mattered because I was a man on a mission. I entered the door to the building and was immediately greeted by a freckled face, stocky security guard with a less than thrilled expression.

"Hello, I am here to see Brenda Ramirez at Imperial Games." "Third floor," he said with an ice-cold demeanor. "Okay, thank you." I continued walking to the elevator. "Wait," He quickly stopped me, so I turned around. "You need to sign the book and I need to see your ID." "Okay, no problem." I signed the book with my initials and gave him a sarcastic smile. I walked into the elevator and proceeded to the third floor. The doors opened and I stepped out and made my way through a dark hallway and followed the light. I made a right down a short corridor and there waiting to greet me was a young African American woman at Imperial's front desk.

"Hi, my name is Joaquin, I am here to see Brenda Ramirez." "Please have a seat," she replied with a bored tone. I sat in one of two Barcelona chairs next to a couple of television consoles with video game systems connected to both. One had a PS4 and the other an Xbox Series S console with Imperial's games on the screens. I sat and watched as workers passed by in T-shirts and jeans while I sat suffocated in a black fitted Prada jacket and shirt. A gift from an ex, the one good thing that came from that relationship. I felt out of place with what I was wearing but I knew this company was definitely for me because I had yet to work somewhere where I had to dress up for a nine-to-five job.

Twenty minutes had gone by while I waited for Brenda to appear. Suddenly, a very pregnant Latina emerged through the glass doors. She looked familiar and had massive, barely covered tits that greeted me with a plunging neckline, but her stomach was like a semi-truck heading straight for me. "Hi, I am Brenda," she said. "Hi, Brenda, it's a pleasure to meet you." We walked through the office and past a room where many of the employees were spread out in front of television screens playing video games. We headed to a conference room in the back of the office, which was splashed in modern décor. It had a huge LED screen on the wall and every video game system attached to it. I sat down on the leather sofas and was prepared for Brenda to ask me anything. With my resume in hand, she scanned over it and began the interrogation.

"The office assistant position requires heavy multitasking; how do you feel about grunt work?" "I'm used to it. My current position and my bartending both require their share of grunt work. I am no stranger to hard work, and I always get the job done. I've had internships in the past where I had to support teams and executives and know what it takes to make an office run smoothly." She seemed to like that response. "I see you've done some acting," she said. "Yes, I've been pursuing my acting career." "This job will take up a majority of your time and there won't be time to go to auditions. We need someone who will be dedicated and will be here for a while," she said. "I understand and yes, I am definitely dedicated." "It's tough being an actor, here you'll make steady money, and you'll have the chance to do voiceovers for the video games." "Okay, sounds good."

All of a sudden, we heard a yell coming from a nearby office. "Brenda! Where are you?!" The man's voice erupted. "Are you easily offended?" "No, not at all I said." "Good, excuse me, I'm sorry." She walked out of the conference room and closed the door behind her. There was utter silence. Fifteen minutes later, she returned. "I apologize for keeping you waiting," she said as she took a deep breath and sat down again. "Brenda! These cashews are salted! I said raw, unsalted!" the voice shouted again. She remained seated as if zoning out the voice. "Joaquin, this job would require a lot from you. We will depend on you heavily for many things." She looked at me as if I was going to rescue her from her hell. "I don't have a problem with that at all. I am highly dependable and responsible." She continued to look at my resume with her legs crossed and her face in a daze while her mind seemed somewhere else. "The salary for the position is $55,000. Does that work for you?" "Yes, that's the range I was seeking." "I think we are done here. I will be in touch with you soon." she said. "Great. Thank you." She walked me out of the office. I walked beside her as we made our way through the corridor. I noticed a wall of glass that I hadn't seen before. Inside, I saw a very muscular man with a shaved head, dark beard and both arms were covered in tattoos. His eyes, filled with anger, followed my every move. "Thank you so much. I will be in touch with you soon," she said.

I walked through the doors and exited the office. The thought didn't escape me that I knew Brenda from somewhere. I couldn't place her, but it drove me crazy that she looked so familiar. I entered the elevator and wondered if I landed the job. I returned to my car and luckily it was still there. I drove and hit traffic immediately. The vehicles surrounded me like a pack of hyenas. I was at a standstill and I couldn't help but to think that this is when I would call Vaughn and tell him about my interview. Instead, a tear ran down my cheek as I tried to remain strong. I finally arrived at my building and ran into my lazy super who was a dead ringer for Mr. Clean except he was a haggard sixty-year-old with sagging muscles and moobs. Yet he showcased his body in tight, dirty wife beaters. "Earl, can you please fix the tiles in my shower? They are falling apart." "When are ya gonna be home?" "I will be home for the rest of the day." "I'll come on Monday," he said as he rushed into his apartment. "Today, Earl! Today!" Knowing he would avoid me for a week before anything was done, I walked up to my apartment. "Ah, home sweet home." I walked straight to my fridge, where I had ten bottles of water and six no salt low-fat cottage cheese pints. I grabbed a bottle of water, when my phone pinged. I had a voicemail, so I began listening to the message I had received while I was driving home. I removed my shoes and jumped onto my bed. I stared at the ceiling. "Hi, Joaquin, It's Brenda Ramirez from Imperial. I wanted to know if you would be able to start on Monday. Please call me back ASAP and let me know." The end of the message synchronized with my smile. I closed my eyes, held a confident grin as I checked a few other messages I had. "Joaquin, honey. It's Marie. You didn't get the part. I was pulling for you, but they went with some Argentinian actor with light hair and blue eyes. I think maybe you should consider a stage name. Think about it sweetie."

Not the kind of messages I like to get from my agent, but I was getting used to it although it didn't make it easier. I continued on to the next message. "Hey, Joaquin, it's Will. I just wanted to know if you could pick up a shift tonight. I know I haven't been to work in a couple of weeks because of drama with my wife, but it would be nice to see you. Anyway, let me know, I hope to see you."

It was always good to hear from Will. There is nothing like a closeted bi-sexual, Latino man with six-pack abs and tattoos to take the edge off my personal life. He was married to a woman and we used to sleep together before Vaughn and I became serious. I never told Vaughn that I used to sleep with my boss because he would have wanted me to quit. He had no clue. I decided to call Brenda back an hour later to avoid sounding desperate. I wanted her to feel like she needed me, not the other way around. "Hello, Brenda, it's Joaquin. I received your message and I wanted to say that, yes, I accept your offer." "Great! Can you start on Monday?" she asked, unable to hide her urgency. "Yes, I can." "Fabulous, I will see you then. Please be here by 9:30 a.m."

"Will do." She hung up and I placed the phone down. I was finally able to leave the dusty dungeon of the library and work in the video game industry. It wasn't Hollywood but it was one step closer. Time to celebrate. I peeled off my clothes and put my gym gear on, grabbed my bottle of water, and left to have a much-needed workout but I had to text Will first. *Hi, Will, yes, I can work. I'll see you tonight.* I called my boss at the library. I knew I would get his voicemail, so I left a message. "Hi Garrett, this is Joaquin. I wanted to let you know that I quit. I'm sorry for the short notice but I found another job and I need to start right away. Thanks."

That evening, I arrived at The Back Door for my bartending shift and immediately ran into Will. Everyone who was scheduled to work was on the floor. As soon as I walked in, Will stepped away from the bar and told me to follow him downstairs to his office. "It's so good to see you," he said. "Same here, you have been M.I.A." "My wife is nagging the shit out of me. It's exhausting. You know, marriage drama." "No, I don't know but that's understandable," I said. "How have you been?" "My boyfriend and I broke up, I got a new job, and I start on Monday, so I'll have to stop working here." "So, you're single and you're leaving?"

Sex between Will and I was always passionate, but I always made sure not to get attached. He was a married man with a child and every gay man in West Hollywood who frequented The Back Door, wanted him. I always knew to enjoy it for what it was and at the same time, maintain discretion, which he appreciated because no one knew we were sleeping with each other.

"It's a good step for me and hopefully for my future." "I understand but I can't say that I am happy about it. I'm happy for you but you are one of the best bartenders I have. I want you to do what's best for you." "Are you going to miss me?" I asked. "I'm going to miss your mouth. My wife can't do what you do." "Well, I haven't been doing that for a while, for you, so I'm sure you haven't been waiting for me to do it." He sat at his desk shirtless, the required attire for workers at The Back Door, with his arms folded as he remained silent with his eyes gazing straight at me. He stood up, walked towards me, grabbed me by the back of my neck, and kissed me. "Does this mean we have to stop this?" he asked. "No, we don't but now we actually have to make an effort to see each other. It's no longer going to be easy." He smiled. "With you, it's always easy." "Fuck off," I said as we both broke out in laughter. He grabbed me by the front of my throat, pushed me against the wall and we started kissing each other aggressively. He unbuckled my belt and unzipped my jeans and stripped me of my boxer briefs. He turned me around and plastered me against the wall. He kissed the back of my neck and passionately began biting it. We heard someone coming down the stairs and he quickly locked the door. "Will, are you there?" The barback asked. "I'm in a meeting!" He spat on his fingers and began lubricating my ass and he was inside. "Ahhhhh-hh," I said in pain. "Take it, I am not going to stop," he whispered. His slow, shallow thrusts became faster and deeper as he pressed me harder against the wall. He continued until he ejaculated inside of me. He was done.

He sat down on his chair. I grabbed my jeans off of the floor, put them on and took off my shirt. He pulled up his jeans quickly. "That was amazing," he said. "Yeah, it was." "Now get to work, I'll be up in ten minutes." I left his office and closed the door behind me. I paused and could hear him pick up his phone to call his wife. Like clockwork, he did this every time we had sex, because he felt guilty. "Hey, honey, how are you? How is Jarod? Yeah, put him on." He began talking to his three-year old son. I walked up the stairs and worked my weekend shift. I would never see Will again.

CHAPTER 4

FIRST DAY
YEAR ONE

I walked into my new job wearing blue jeans, a short-sleeve fitted black, button-down black shirt and my black Converse sneakers. I said hello to the security guard, and he stopped me immediately. "Can I help you?" he asked. "I work for Imperial now, today is my first day." "Whatever, go." I entered the elevator surrounded by five heavy, geeky types who looked like they forgot to bathe today. I realized they must be game testers. They don't get out much apparently. One of them spoke to the guy nearest the doors. "Did you play the new *Call of Duty*?" "Yeah, I went through it in six hours" I knew that game well. An unemployed ex of mine smoked weed and played that game non-stop. The elevator took an eternity to arrive at the third floor. I walked into the office behind them, and they looked at me like I was a foreigner entering a world where I wasn't welcome.

The receptionist had transformed herself into Missy Elliott circa 1997. Her hair was styled with finger waves in the front and a ponytail in the back. I wondered if she would rap for me. All of a sudden, I couldn't get Missy Elliott's song "The Rain (Supa Dupa Fly)" out of my head. "Hey, boo, I'm Aisha," she said. She appeared to be in a much better mood than last time. "Hi, Aisha, it's nice to meet you." "Brenda told me to show you how things are done at the reception desk since you'll be covering for me when I go to lunch." This was going to be interesting. The education began. The phone rang and she picked it up. "Imperial Games, how can I help you?" "Hold on," she said as she rolled her eyes and transferred the call to someone in the office. She proceeded to educate me. "Ok, it's important for you to know where the supplies are because someone may need you to ship something, and this is where you'll find it." She opened a closet door that housed all of the FedEx boxes. It was completely chaotic. The boxes, in a variety of sizes, were piled on the ground creating what resembled an art installation called laziness. Banksy it was not. I am sure she was the one who flung them in there to avoid breaking one of her glitter polished talons. She closed the door to the closet. The phone began to ring. She looked at me and told me to hold up and rolled her eyes again. "Hello, hey girl. Whatcha doing? Giirrl, you know they got me stressed out. I'm here training people and shit. "Yeah, giirrl, I'll see you at lunch, I'm starving, I haven't gotten a chance to eat a thing." I stood there in amazement and in doubt. It was 11:00 a.m. and she was about five feet, nine inches tall with around 250 pounds on her. I'm positive she had already eaten. "I'll talk to you later, girl. I gotta go." She hung up the phone and reached for something under the counter. A cinnamon raisin bagel, half eaten, slathered in cream cheese and grape jelly. I laughed to myself.

The phone rang again but as it did, Brenda entered the office stomach first. It seemed as though every part of her body had grown, except her ass. It was an ironing board. "Hi, Joaquin, how are you?" She said as she attempted to catch her breath. "Hi, Brenda, I'm fine thanks and yourself?" "Traffic was a nightmare this morning. Come to my desk." I completed my first phase of training, Aisha 101. "I'll finish showing you the phone system when you come back," Aisha said with her mouth full as she gnawed on her bagel. I gladly walked over to Brenda's desk. I noticed that the door to this area of the office was shattered. "How was your weekend?" I asked. "It was good, thanks, basically I relaxed with my husband and felt like a beached whale. I can't wait to give birth. It's so weird seeing my fucking body change like this again. Back in the day, I used to be a skinny bitch doing lines of coke at The Roxbury and now I'm pregnant and living in Orange County worrying about the lines on my face. I am married to a tool who still dreams that he and his friends are going to be the next Maroon 5. Let me give you some advice on a personal level. Marry for money. Fuck love. That shit only works out in the movies. I didn't marry a businessman. You want to know who I married? I married a man who I fell in love with and after we got married, all of a sudden, he had no drive or ambition but to be a singer with his band. I met him in Vegas, and now he is thirty-five years old and expects me to step it up when I make more money than the son of a bitch." I stood there thinking, Wow, this is Monday morning. My first day, I was ambushed by Missy Elliott and now I have become a therapist to a woman who should be cast on *The Real Housewives of Orange County*. "I'm sorry, you must think I'm crazy, it's the hormones," she said. "No, not at all, don't worry about it."

I looked around the office and it was practically empty with the exception of the game testers I saw arrive earlier. Apparently, the video game industry doesn't require its employees to start the day early. "Brenda, why is the office so empty?" "Most of them were here until 3:00 a.m. *Homicide III* will be released in a few months, so they have no choice. It's Mike's baby and our biggest game, so unless they want to deal with Mike going on his own crime spree and bashing their heads just before he fires them, they deal with it. He expects everyone, except us, to be here seven days a week but I have to be on-call during the weekends. I don't give a shit about the game or them but if the game does well, we do well and I shower myself with Birkin bags," she said as she pointed to her massive Birkin resting on her desk. "I also avoid the effects of stress thanks to my 'tox." "'Tox?" "Botox, I can't wait to pop this baby out so I can smooth out these lines." She looked at herself in a compact mirror. I could only smile as I found Brenda entertaining. She held her stomach and leaned back embracing the globe.

"Ok, let me show you around the office before Mike, Imperial's president and founder comes in. I like to call him the Kraken." "Kraken?" I laughed. "Yeah, when he comes into the office, you'll see why. He sits back there." She pointed to the office I walked past before as I remembered the face of the intense man with the shaved head who gave me the evil eye. With a better perspective of the office, it reminds me of Hannibal Lecter's enclosure in *The Silence of The Lambs*. A portion of the glass was shattered almost as if a caged animal couldn't take the madness anymore. "Brenda, what happened to the glass?" "Oh, that was Friday afternoon and that was Friday evening," she said casually as she pointed in the direction of the office door. "Let's go to the kitchen." We walked into a small kitchen in which I was responsible for making sure all of the supplies remained fully stocked. "This is the company trough. We have snacks, beverages for the employees at all times since they never leave." We walked out of the kitchen and she proceeded to show me the rest of the office and introduced me to other employees. We walked through the glass doors and entered another set of doors that led to the marketing and art departments. Everyone sat at their desks consumed by their computer screens. They appeared to be in a trance. Brenda wasn't kidding when she said they never left. Many of them looked like they were in dire need of a shower. I was clearly not working somewhere where the men cared about their appearance.

We entered an office where two women were both on the telephone. As we entered, the one with the platinum blonde straight hair, waif-like body, and a visible tattoo of a snake on her forearm turned to us as she hung up the phone. "Joaquin, I'd like you to meet Christina. She is our VP of Operations," Brenda said. "Hi, it's a pleasure to meet you," I said. "Welcome to Imperial Games. I'm sure you are going to like it here." Not a minute later, her phone rang as well as her iPhone. "I'm sorry, I have to take this," she said. "She rarely gets to see the light of day." Brenda whispered to me. Just as Christina took the call, on the opposite side of her was someone who was introduced to me as Annabel. Where Christina was a pale, rail thin New Yorker, made obvious by her accent, Annabel was a pale rail thin Australian. She hung up after wrapping up her call. "Hello, Joaquin. I am sure we will be keeping you busy," she said in an Australian accent. I smile, "Well, I am looking forward to it." We exited their office. "I'm convinced those bitches are on the Calvin Klein diet of hot water, lemon, and Cocaine. There is no way they can look like that and eat the way they do. Trust me, I should know." It appeared as if some of the women of this company left the fashion industry and settled into the realms of heavy, unattractive, frumpy men. Maybe they were here because they didn't have to compete for attention. The guys probably looked at them as goddesses and they didn't have to feel insecure about anything. Brenda continued to walk me around and I was amazed at how the workers continued to be hypnotized by their computer screens. They weren't moving at all as we walked by. I wonder what would happen if they looked away, maybe they would get shot.

We continued to walk down a hallway that led us to another office. "This is August Brown's office. He is the Chief Marketing Officer." She knocked on the door. "Come in," a voice said from inside. "Hi, August, I would like you to meet our new office assistant, Joaquin Otero." August turned around in his leather BoConcept chair. He was a chubby, tall guy with black thinned out hair, a scruffy face. He stood up to shake my hand. "Hi, dude, welcome to our empire," he said. "Alright, we'll leave you to your work," Brenda said. "Thanks, we are glad to have you here, Joaquin, we need a lot of organization. These guys are fucking pigs." "Thanks, it's a pleasure to meet you," I said. Brenda and I walked out of his office and continued on to the other side where there were two large cubicles with the occupants not yet in them.

"The office in the corner, near the window belongs to Mike's sister, Rachael Chapman. She's a piece of work, her and Mike are always fighting, and that office belongs to Gavin Kent. He is Mike's bitch. If they weren't straight, I'd swear they were fucking," she said. I looked inside Rachael's office, and everything was drowning under piles of clutter. Definitely not something you'd expect from a woman's office. Then I took a quick glance at Gavin's area and it was extremely meticulous with a dog crate on the side of his desk with a Louis Vuitton throw resting on a chair. His desk contained a MacBook Pro and a bottle of Burberry cologne resting on the glass top. The center of the glass was blanketed by remnants of a white substance which I am sure wasn't baby powder. "Brenda!" There was that voice again. The voice that could only belong to Mike Chapman. Brenda's face became visibly tense, despite the Botox. "There's the beast," she said. She directed me to a storage closet near Christina and Annabel's office and quickly opened the door. "Get started organizing this room and I will be back in a bit," she said. "Okay, no problem," I said. She rushed out as quickly as a pregnant woman could.

I was in a room the size of a medium walk-in-closet. T-shirts were thrown and piled everywhere, on the shelves and the floor. I folded the shirts one by one and arranged them by size. My part-time job at Urban Outfitters, when I was in college, was going to pay off. Brenda finally reached the other side of the office. She walked into Mike's office and stepped on shards of glass as she likely was momentarily daydreaming about a frozen Margarita at happy hour. However, there was nothing happy about this hour and there were no drinks in sight. The glass was from his office door. The stainless steel exterior now had a gaping hole in it where there was frosted glass as of fifteen minutes prior. "Where were you?" "I was giving our new office assistant a tour of the office." "You know to be at your desk when I arrive. Don't you understand I am under a lot of pressure right now? I need you to go to Starbucks and get me my Nitro Cold Brew then go to Whole Foods and get me raw cashews, Quest Protein Bars, and Asian pears. Make sure the cashews are raw and unsalted and that the pears are hard, don't bring me mushy shit." "Is there anything else?" "Yes, have this mess cleaned up immediately and have this door repaired and the other one." "Sure thing," she replied with a fake smile. Brenda walked out of his office and called the office's Peruvian cleaning lady to take care of it. "Lupita, aquí, rápido, rápido," she said. Lupita rushed over. "Limpia esto ahora por favor." Brenda conveyed as she pointed to the mess on the floor. "No problema," Lupita said. Brenda bolted out of the office to fulfill Mike's request. The closet I was working on started to become organized but with over one thousand T-shirts to go, I was there for a while. "Who the hell are you?" I turned around and a brunette woman was standing there wearing a tailored, fitted pantsuit. She had a combination of feminine and masculine traits to her but leaned on the butch side. "I am Joaquin, I am the new office assistant. Today is my first day." "Great, just what we need around here, another man. I am Rachael Chapman, the Chief Creative Officer." "Oh, you're Mike's sister. It's a pleasure to meet you." She grimaced, "Yeah, that's me. I need your help dude. I need two men's large, black *Homicide* tees and one lady's medium for my cunt of an assistant who finally did something right so I will throw her a bone," she said nonchalantly as she stared at her iPhone. I pretended I didn't hear the remark and handed her the T-shirts she requested. "Here you go." "Thanks man and welcome," she said as she continued to look at her phone and walked out. I kept working on the shirts and knew it was going to take me the rest of the day.

CHAPTER 5

MULTIPLAYER

My alarm sounded off at 6:00 a.m. so I could make it to the gym. One of the perks of my new job was that all the employees received free memberships to Equinox as of day one. I wasted no time. I took full advantage of that and planned to head there every morning before work. Even at twenty-five, I still had to maintain a twenty-nine-inch waist. Low carbs, high protein, add free-weights into the equation and that summed up my mornings. In the fashion and entertainment industries, taking care of your appearance was just as important as your resume. I quickly noticed, in the video game industry, the larger your waistline, hair loss, premature wrinkles, dark circles under your eyes and double chins, the more you were a team player and were rewarded immensely. I, however, was not going to fall victim to that epidemic. The closest I was going to get to the video games was doing a voiceover, seeing them played by the testers or overhearing the marketing department strategize their plans for the upcoming game. I was fine with that. They had all aged before their time and received the same perks I did, and I left the office at

6:00 p.m. while they departed five to eight hours later. This was a pit stop on my journey and I knew I had to make the most of it.

After the gym, I headed to the office and settled into my daily routine. I walked in and said hello to Aisha, who always greeted me with her signature "Hey Boo" and a new hairstyle every week. I looked forward to Mondays because I wondered what she would do next. She had a new hairstyle and nails to match and sometimes the colors matched perfectly. I walked through the corridor and straight to the kitchen. I noticed that all the glass had been replaced from the previous day's drama. It was as if Mike's tantrum never occurred and that was how he liked his employees to treat them as well. I made my rounds, first stop was the kitchen where I filled up the fridge with sodas, of all varieties, and made certain they were all straight with the brand facing forward. Those were the specific instructions Brenda had given me. I stocked up the coffee cups, utensils, napkins and placed a new jug of spring water in the water dispenser. The kitchen was finished and ready to be ransacked so that I could fix it all over again. As I walked out of the kitchen, I headed back to Aisha's desk to see if there were any packages that needed to be distributed. There was a stack from FedEx and UPS so I walked around the office and tried to decipher who they belonged to, with Aisha's guidance, and at the same time getting to know the other employees. After I distributed the packages, Brenda arrived and asked me to come see her. "Joaquin, you did an excellent job with the storage closet. The T-shirts look amazing. I now need you to organize Mike's archive of games." She opened the door to another closet filled with video games for every console, DVDs and CDs. The collection consisted of Imperial's own games and those of other competitors as well. "Can you organize all of these alphabetically?" I had a feeling this was a project Mike asked her to do, but she decided to pass it on to me.

As I began, Brenda sat down and held her stomach as if it were a crystal ball and it was going to give her clarity about her life. Mike arrived in the office and didn't say a word and gave me a dirty look as he walked by. "Brenda!" he summoned. "Yes?" she said in a daze. Her eyes spoke volumes as she entered his office. "Why is that guy touching my stuff?" he asked her in a whisper, but I still heard him as his door was wide open. "Joaquin did such a great job with the T-shirt closet; I thought it would be great for him to organize your archive." "I asked you to do that weeks ago," he said agitated. "Don't worry, it's going to look great, and everything will be exactly the way you want it." I watched from the corner of my eye as he calmed down a bit. Brenda had a motherly aspect about her that made him feel better about things. I organized the games as if I didn't hear a word of what was said. I continued my daily routine for three months. Mindless office projects, making my rounds around the office, making sure the copiers and printers were fed with reams of paper and that the office ran smoothly. If things were in order, it was thanks to me. I would have to constantly re-organize the T-shirt closet because someone would always go in there and create a disaster or we would get new shipments that illustrated Imperial's inflated marketing budget. Brad, Christina's Production Assistant, was from Portland and in his early twenties. He had been working at Imperial for a year and looked like he was pushing thirty-five due to his prematurely balding head. He wasn't attractive but someone must have told him he had to have a fit body because of it. His insecurity would always force him to wear a baseball cap. I would often help him with receiving shipments of T-shirts and coordinating the distribution of them. However, at the same time, Brenda gave me additional responsibilities of doing small tasks or projects for Mike. When Mike needed me to run an errand or work on an organizational project, everything else had to be dropped because Mike was always priority number one.

On one particular Friday afternoon, Brad said he was going to need my help with a shipment that was arriving. I told him I couldn't help him because I had to run an errand for Mike. Brenda and I had to go to a storage facility to add more items for Mike's archive. Mike collected ten of everything. Promotional giveaways, games, T-shirts, I mean everything associated with the company's games. This created a lot of work for Brenda and now me, collecting all the materials and then storing it offsite. He either suffered from severe hoarding or he planned on opening a museum someday. I believed he was a hoarder. Brad wasn't happy that I couldn't help him because he had to deal with the entire shipment on his own.

A few days later, I ran into August in the elevator who told me he heard great things about me. I was doing a great job in a short time and he proceeded to ask me questions of where I had worked in the past and he requested to see my resume. He told me there was a position opening up in the PR department and he thought I might be a great fit for it. I was excited about the possibility of moving into the PR department after three months at the company. This position would allow me to have access to media contacts. Although I didn't want to be a publicist, I knew someday I would have one of my own, so it was a chance to learn the inner workings of what they did. The following day, I woke up, flew out of bed, pumped and motivated to hit the gym hard. I walked into the office with excitement, thinking that after three months of mundane tasks, this could be my chance to make big changes which could benefit my career. I continued my usual office routine but this time with the mindset that I wouldn't have to do it much longer.

When Charles Santos, the PR director, arrived at the office, he said he wanted to speak to me in about twenty minutes. They were a long twenty minutes but finally Charles asked me to join him in the conference room. "Joaquin, I have heard great things about you and August mentioned to me

that he thinks you may be a great fit for the PR department."
"Thank you, I'm glad to hear that. I think it would be the right move for me and am looking forward to expanding in that direction." "I understand at some point, you were an entertainment correspondent for a website." "Yes, I conducted on-camera interviews with actors, actresses, directors of independent films and theater shows. Unfortunately, it wasn't a full-time position, and the website went out of business." "It's great that you had that kind of exposure from that perspective." He continued to ask me more questions and the interview was over.

I was confident and felt that I was definitely going to be promoted. I already envisioned my desk which would be the empty one on the corner nearest to the T-shirt closet. I stopped my daydreaming and returned to my daily tasks. Two weeks had passed by and I hadn't heard anything. I would see Charles in the hallway, and he would smile, yet not mention anything about the role. I was confused and didn't understand why I hadn't heard good news from him. During this period of time, my bond with Brenda had grown closer. I believe it all started when she vented to me about her husband and all of a sudden, we had a connection. She pulled me aside on a Wednesday afternoon and she said she had to speak to me about something. "I know you have been anxious to hear back about the PR position, but I wanted to let you know that you aren't going to get it." "Why?" I asked, disappointed. "Brad told August that you have an attitude problem and that you would be a liability to the PR team. Brad got it into August's head, and it shut the door on your chances." "That's ridiculous, he must still be pissed because I was running errands for Mike, the day he wanted me to help him with the shipment." "I know you were looking to get into that department but don't worry. Mike likes you and you will have more responsibility working with us. We will give you more projects and that will allow you to work more with him." I said to myself, *I don't want to work with that maniac. I don't care if he is the president of the company.* "Alright, thanks." I said in the most appreciative tone I could muster at the moment. I had to get used to sodas, copy paper and sorting mail.

I didn't approach Brad about it at all. I held on to that piece of information and made sure I would repay him later. "I am going on maternity leave in a few weeks and Mike is definitely going to need more attention. I am hiring a temp but I am sure that won't be enough so you will definitely stand out." "Thanks Brenda," I said as I returned back to work but wasn't interested in becoming Mike's assistant. I didn't have the personality for it and my ambition wouldn't allow me to consider it.

A few days later, I walked into the office and noticed that Brenda was in earlier than usual sitting at her desk with an eager looking young woman. "Good morning, Brenda." "Good morning, Joaquin. I'll speak to you in a second, I'm training Stacy, our new temp." I continued with my work until noon when Brenda had a chance to speak to me. "Mike called out sick today. He rarely does that, but I am sure you noticed that the office is a lot less tense when he is not around. I'm hoping Stacy will be able to deal with Mike while I am on maternity leave." She trained Stacy for the rest of the day. On Friday, Mike returned. I was in the kitchen stocking the fridge when I heard him enter the office. "Brenda, in my office now." He walked past Brenda's desk and his presence visibly intimidated Stacy. She wore a low-cut sweater exposing her cleavage no doubt hoping to win him over. "Good morning Mr. Chapman." Mike ignored her as he walked past. I stood by Mike's office and overheard him saying he wanted Stacy gone. Brenda tried to convince him otherwise. "Get rid of her now! I don't want some random person taking care of my personal shit." This time the whole office heard him, and Stacy was frozen at her computer as she waited for Brenda to return. I decided to hang around the reception area and pretend I was organizing the mail.

In the meantime, I heard Aisha on the phone explaining to a friend that her man Dashawn is a playa and thank God he isn't the baby daddy to any of her three kids. She would periodically be interrupted by incoming calls and she transferred them, annoyed they were interrupting her. All of a sudden, the office door swung open and Stacy rushed out crying. "Have a nice day." I said. I knew she would be too weak to work here but we'll see what happens with the next one. "What happened?" Aisha asked me as she paused from her important call. "It doesn't matter," I said.

I returned to Brenda's desk. "I have to speak to you," Brenda said. We walked over to the conference room and my mind started racing. *Am I being laid off? At least I would get unemployment. Is Mike angry with me? Did I do something wrong?* I sat down in the same spot where I interviewed for the position, except now I could possibly be told that I was no longer needed. I knew one thing; I definitely wouldn't be walking out in tears. "I brought you in here to let you know that Mike decided he doesn't want me to bring in a temp. He doesn't trust someone new coming in and handling his needs while I am gone." "Ok," I replied, still confused and waiting to hear what the rest of the story was. "We discussed it and he would like you to assist him while I am on maternity leave." I sat there speechless and not knowing exactly what to say. I mean, what was I supposed to say? *Thanks for giving me the chance to work for a psycho for the next three months, I couldn't have asked for a better opportunity.* Brenda noticed that I was speechless and quickly followed up with the magic words. "You would have your pay generously increased, effective immediately." That quickly changed my expression. "I'm in." "You will still be responsible for your current tasks but when Mike needs you, he takes priority." At the same time, I kept telling myself, this asshole was not going to break me down. I would be able to handle his bullshit.

"Oh Joaquin, before I forget, this is a non-disclosure agreement Mike needs you to sign before you begin working with him. It is standard, read it over, sign it and give it back to me." "Ok, no problem." At that very moment, Lupita was wiping down the side of Brenda's desk and the cabinets on the side. "Hola Lupita, ¿cómo estas?" I asked and smiled. "Hola mijo, bien gracias, y tú? "Bien gracias." "Me alegro," she said. "OMG!" Brenda yelled.

I looked up from reading the document as Brenda stood and her water broke all over her flip flops. I placed the agreement down. "Oh my God, my water broke, oh shit, what am I going to do?" She had the attention of the entire office. Brenda was definitely on high drama, which for her was normal but she was really over the top at the moment. "Ay dios mío. Viene el bebé, viene el bebé," Lupita shouted as she was more panicked than Brenda and they were feeding off of each other's energy. "What the hell is going on here?" Mike asked. "Brenda's water just broke," one of the testers responded. "Everyone back to work." Mike shouted and everyone scattered. Lupita lingered at a nearby desk as she pretended to clean, while paying close attention as if her favorite telenovela was on. "My doctor is in Orange County. This can't be happening," Brenda said loudly. "Fuck! I can't believe you are doing this to me now. You weren't supposed to have that baby until next week. I wasn't prepared to have you leave yet," Mike said. "I am having a fucking baby and am one week overdue and you didn't want me to work from home, so this is what happens you asshole," she erupted. "Great, now you're going to blame this on me," he said. "Brenda, get ahold of yourself. Call Marek and have him take you to the hospital," Mike said. Marek, Mike's driver, was always on call whenever Mike needed him. Although he attempted to be helpful, Mike couldn't help but be himself. Mike looked at me, "Jason, get her things and help her down to the car. I am not sure she will make it down in this hysterical state." "It's called pregnancy and his name is Joaquin," Brenda said. The whole office was there as they witnessed the exchange between him and Brenda. "Go, go already," he directed us out annoyed. Brenda walked quickly to the elevators. "Brenda, I'll be right back, I forgot something," I said. "Lupita, limpia el escritorio y rompe esos papeles en el shredder," I said. I wanted to make sure she cleaned up the mess at Brenda's desk and threw away the unnecessary clutter on top of her desk, including shredding the non-disclosure agreement.

I continued on to the elevators with Brenda as she clutched on my arm for support with one hand and she held onto her new Birkin with her other hand. "I know you will do fine assisting Mike while I am gone. I will call to see if you need help with anything and I'll have my phone with me." The elevator ride seemed like an eternity. Marek was in the area so he was already waiting in the lobby. He grabbed Brenda by the arm and reached for her Birkin, so she didn't have to carry it. She slapped his hand away as if he was about to take her child from her. I couldn't help but smile. She stepped into the SUV and lowered the window. "Whenever things get rough, just remember, it's all about the money. The more he trusts you and the more information you know, the more he is going to pay you. Keep that in mind, especially on days when you feel like walking away." The window rolled up and the SUV drove off. I walked back into the building and straight into the open elevator. I stood thinking to myself in silence. All of a sudden, I heard a voice in the elevator coming from the speaker. "You are so dead. You'll be gone in a week." It was the rude security guard downstairs. "Fuck off," I said as I looked into the camera. That was the kind of thick skin I needed to have in order to survive in the office.

I walked out of the elevator and headed back to Brenda's desk. Lupita had cleaned everything up, it was as if Brenda's fiasco never occurred, and the desk was spotless. I looked in Mike's office and he had the shade down and his door was closed. He didn't want to be bothered. I acquainted myself with Brenda's files to get an idea of what needed to be done. I tried to make sense of everything but there were a lot of disorganized documents and many of them were her personal things. An hour passed and Mike hadn't emerged from his office. I hoped he would stay there for the next three months. I made sure that I had Outlook open so I wouldn't miss any emails but there weren't any. So far, so good.

I looked under Brenda's desk and noticed a large stack of magazines. I grabbed them and realized they were old fashion publications from the '80s. *Vogue, Elle, Cosmopolitan, Vogue Italia, Mademoiselle*, the list was endless. I thought they were things that needed to be recycled but when I glanced at the covers, I noticed Brenda was on the cover of all of them. Mike finally exited his office, and I threw the magazines back under the desk. "Jason, I'm stepping out to a meeting." "Okay, Mike, just so you know, my name is Joaquin." "I know but I don't like your name, I thought Jason was better. How about I call you J?" "Sure." "Before I forget, here are my house keys, meet with my cleaning lady at 1:00 p.m. in front of my house in Hancock Park. My address is in Brenda's contacts and my cleaning lady's name is Ana." He handed me $250. "You will need to stay there until she is done," he said as he flung his keys on to the desk. I had a few hours before I had to meet with Ana, so I kept exploring Brenda's desk when the phone rang. "Mike Chapman's office." "Joaquin, oooh, oooh. It's me Brenda. I had to sneak this call in while the nurse stepped away. They are waiting for me to be fully dilated. My husband is running late because he was rehearsing with his fucking band and Mike keeps emailing me. I have one man at home who doesn't understand what I have been through in the past nine months while I carry his child, and another man who acts like a baby who doesn't understand I can't hold his hand while I am squeezing a real baby out of my thirty-five-year-old vagina."

Brenda was on one of her rants, so I humored her and also went along with the fact she was thirty-five when I knew she was really forty. "Anyway, he emailed me to let you know a couple of things. First, make sure you aren't late when meeting with Ana and in the coming months don't forget to ask him for her money because he often forgets when she is supposed to come. She gets $200." "He gave me $250." "He is testing you and likes doing that so stay on your toes. He would love for you to fuck up. It gives him an excuse to explode. Also, always make sure to take your lunch at the same time every day and take it. He is a creature of habit and gets used to your schedule.

One more thing, I know you go to the gym in the morning, but Mike is starting to work out with the trainer at the gym in the mornings as well. He doesn't want you working out there at the same time he does so go to the gym during your lunch hour. He saw you at the gym last week and was pissed." "Why? What's the big deal?" "Although the gym is a company perk, Mike doesn't want to see employees working out when he is there because he feels they should be working, and it distracts him from his workout." "Ok, I'll go during my lunch hour." "By the way, open the black filing cabinet to the right of my desk. In it, you will find instructions on how Mike likes things done. Make sure to read it thoroughly. He updates it and will hand you a new one every few weeks or so because he adds more demands. Then you will have to shred the document when he hands you a new one. In the back of the filing cabinet, you will find a little box that will definitely come in handy. Ooh, the nurse is coming, I have to go." After I hung up with Brenda, I looked in the filing cabinet for the document she mentioned. I couldn't miss it. It was a large document that looked more like a script. The title of the document read The Bible According to Mike. The importance of the document was emphasized by the word "Confidential" watermarked across the pages. *Jesus, this is a manual of how to manage his life, likes and dislikes.* It also included a list of people who were blacklisted. It included people whose calls he wouldn't take and employees at the company that he would never be available for. This page was updated weekly to coincide with the turns of the tide. He was very fickle about the employees who, as a whole, he referred to as his "family", but he apparently hated a majority of them. They worked long hours to make him a wealthier man, but they were all disposable in his eyes. This was the gospel according to Mike. I had to read it, memorize and worship it. I opened the first couple of pages to take a quick look at it.

List of Demands

1 - Every two weeks, I will give you an envelope on Fridays, in the early evening. You will take this envelope to an address I will give you in East L.A. Once there, you will ring buzzer #22. Do this at 8:00 p.m. and return to my place to hand me the package.

2 - I bring my dog into the office often. Walk her every hour until she goes. I don't want any accidents inside the office.

3 - Usually on Fridays, unless otherwise instructed, I will ask you to call this number 555-6969 and ask you to tell Shana to be at my house by 10:00 p.m.

4 - I only drink alkaline bottled water. Always make sure my water is refrigerated and ready to hand to me as I walk through the door.

5 - When I ask you to purchase anything, I will expect you to get it immediately.

6 - Don't speak to me unless I speak to you first. If I need anything, I will let you know.

7 - Every morning buy me a Nitro Cold Brew from Starbucks Reserve. You'll have to buy it on your way into the office.

8 - When I ask you to get me food, don't have it delivered. They always take too long. You are required to pick up my food at all times.

9 - All my phone messages are to be typed out and emailed to me. Please include: Name, Number, Time Called and Message.

10 - Always double, triple confirm pick-up times when you have my driver pick me up. I never want to be left waiting.

I memorized one through ten and moved on to the following pages. The list consisted of two hundred items that were a combination of odd and extreme. I am sure things weren't so straightforward in reality. I was expected to study the document. Not one to enjoy studying, I put it down and returned to viewing the old fashion magazines with Brenda on the cover. I wanted to explore how she ended up here if she was a supermodel. I found a portfolio under the magazines. I opened it and saw fashion ads that were familiar to me when I was younger. She wasn't one of the top models of the time like Christie Brinkley or Paulina Porizkova but nonetheless I knew the face. Well, at least the face she had then.

She's had more relationships with a knife than a man. I decided to Google her. She read like an *E True Hollywood Story* except she wasn't famous enough to have one. She never made a dent in Hollywood unless you count her two straight to DVD films listed on IMDb. *The Mistress* and *The Latina.* They sounded like porn titles, I scrolled down to see what else I could find out. She blew most of her money from doing drugs in the 1980s, had two stints in rehab and has two children from previous marriages where both husbands were given full custody. She was an only child and her parents died in a car accident when she was twenty-one. She had been picking up the pieces since. She went bankrupt around the time she began working for Mike, which is when her looks began to fall apart. She was only forty but her hard partying lifestyle in her youth had caught up with her which was why she had resorted to Botox and her addiction to plastic surgery was born. Which is sad because she is Latina and should have aged well. She ended up with her current husband who had no celebrity cred and was a wannabe rock star. According to TMZ's news archive, she was due for another breakdown in a few months. She was in their "What Ever Happened To" section. Maybe her breakdown would come in the form of postpartum depression or maybe she would have a midlife crisis and leave her baby with her cleaning lady who doubled as a nanny while she went clubbing without underwear on. I noticed one of the covers had her and Janice Dickinson posing together. I realized I was losing track of time and it was time for me to meet with Ana.

From what Brenda had told me, Ana had been Mike's cleaning lady for the past four years, and out of his paranoia, had always refused to give her a set of keys. Besides being incredibly successful, Mike suffered from an insane degree of paranoia. Brenda had mentioned that Mike was a pothead so I was sure that couldn't help. I rushed off to Mike's house in Hancock Park. I finally arrived and I saw Ana waiting in her car by the gate. I waved to her and moved into the driveway so I could enter the code. I pulled into the house and Ana followed me with her car. She was an older woman with long auburn hair. "Hola, Ana." "Hola," she said. "Mucho gusto en conocerte. Mi nombre es Joaquín. Yo soy el nuevo asistente ayudando a Mike porque Brenda está en maternity leave." I pulled my cell phone out of my pocket so we could exchange numbers. I noticed the Argentinian flag case on her iPhone case. Argentinian pride, which meant she probably thought she was European and not South American. We walked into Mike's house, I noticed three cats scattering to their hiding places. Ana began to move as quickly as she could because from what I understood, it took her several hours to clean his place because it was so big. I had to sit here and wait until she was done so I decided to walk around and give myself a tour of Mike's home. The two-floor home was modern, but I expected it to be bigger than it was. He had one room that was clearly the game room. It had a pinball machine, ping pong table and several arcade classics. All of a sudden, I was transported to my childhood when I used to go to arcades at the mall. I walked into a library where I was surrounded by books. I looked at the bookshelf and there was *The Exorcist* by William Peter Blatty along with several large books celebrating the works of different photographers. There were French doors that led to the pool area. I opened them and there was a pristine lap pool. I sat down on an outdoor chair to take a moment to take it in.

All of a sudden, my phone began to ring. It was Mike. "Where are you?" he asked. "I'm in your house, Ana is cleaning." "As soon as she's done, go to Lemonade and pick up my lunch. I want the Texas BBQ brisket, white truffle mac 'n' cheese and a Diet Coke." He hung up before I could respond. I went back into the house and Ana had about an hour left. I went upstairs where she was cleaning the bedrooms and walked into the master. It was odd that his home felt so serene because he was anything but. There were several silver picture frames of happy moments that all looked staged. One was of him and his ex-girlfriend. She wasn't interested in him for his money, she actually loved him, and he apparently fucked it up. At least that's what I heard in the office. "Ok, I'm finished," Ana said. I placed the frame down and was ready to get back to the office I escorted Ana out and as she quickly drove out to beat traffic, I followed shortly after in my car watching the gates of hell close behind me. I picked up his food from Lemonade and I hit some traffic, but I made it in forty-five minutes. I ran into the building and the security guard had an angry look on his face. "Slow down," he shouted. It was easy for him to say, he didn't work for the Kraken. As usual the elevator took an eternity especially when I knew Mike was rushing me. I walked into the office. "Mike's lookin' for you. Mmmmm, hmmm, Aisha said while popping her gum. As if I already didn't know. I walked through the corridor and could see Mike's face through the glass. "Bring your laptop," he said. I grabbed it from Brenda's desk and entered his office. I tried to slow myself down once I entered. "What took you so long?" "I'm sorry about that, I hit traffic." "My food better not be cold." He took a bite into his sandwich. "Fuck me, this shit is lukewarm. Nuke it in the microwave and put everything on a plate while you're at it." I grabbed a Diet Coke from the fridge I left in pristine condition, but it was now ransacked.

I returned with his lunch and he grabbed the plate as if it was his last meal ever. "Mike, that reminds me, you gave me $250 earlier to give to Ana and she only gets $200. Here is your change." "Thanks, dude." I handed him his preferred beverage. When I entered his office, I noticed a stench I didn't notice before. I had no idea what it was until I realized it was his gym clothes on the ground. The smell was a familiar scent that you often smell synonymous with Skid Row. Eu de urinal toilette a la homeless man. He didn't seem to believe in showering after the gym. I left his office as quickly as I entered and returned to my desk. There was a brand-new iPhone sitting on top of it. I picked it up puzzled that someone must have left it there by mistake. Mike began tapping the glass and speaking to me with his mouth full. "J, that's yours. Tell Kevin in IT that I said to set it up for you immediately." I didn't need two iPhones but now I have them. Most people would be excited to see a new iPhone on their desk, but I was smarter than that. I knew in Mike's world this was my ankle bracelet. I went to see the IT guys who were only a few steps away from Brenda's desk. Of the three, one of them was in the office sitting below an enormous poster of Jenna Jameson, geeky posters adorned the adjacent walls, and he was glued to the computer screen. I thought he was busy reviewing data but I noticed he was playing one of the *Call of Duty* games. His dirty blond hair looked like it hadn't been washed in days and he was a cross between a geek and a skater. "Hi, are you Kevin?" "Oh shit." He was startled and minimized the video game on his screen. Apparently, he is actually supposed to be doing something else that doesn't involve him playing video games. "Hey, man." He turned around and extended his hand. "I'm Joaquin, we haven't officially met but I am the new office assistant. I am also assisting Mike while Brenda is on maternity leave. Mike said you would set up my iPhone for me." "Sure, I'll have it for you by the end of the day." He grabbed it from me with urgency so he could get back to his game.

I heard Mike's phone ringing and I rushed to answer it. "Mike Chapman's office." A woman who sounded as though she was gasping for air was on the other line. "Hello," I said. "Joaquin, it's me Brenda." "Hi, how are you?" "Don't tell him it's me. Tell him it's Ana if he asks. Also, when you answer his phone, say Imperial Games. He doesn't want people to know they are calling his direct line. Sometimes we get fans that try to call him directly." "Ok, thanks. I'll make sure to do that." "I feel as though my vagina has been stretched like a rubber band. I'll have to get some work done to tighten the girl up again, along with my stomach." *TMI, TMI* I thought. "You're too hard on yourself," I said, trying to make the emotionally fragile Brenda feel better at the moment. "No, hard is what life is. I'm the one recovering from labor and yet my husband is passed out in a chair in front of me with a bag of potato chips in his hand. My life is so fucked up." As I listened to Brenda, I realized I was wearing my therapist hat again. Since she didn't have any family or custody of her kids, her deadbeat husband was all she had. "On top of that, Mike keeps emailing me. He wanted me to let you know to always make sure to keep your new phone on at all times." I noticed Mike began looking at me, probably wondering who I was talking to on one of his lines. I turned to him. "It's Brenda." "Is everything alright?" "Yes, it is." I turned around and continued listening to her. "Okay, I have to go, I have to breastfeed my baby and then my husband right after," she said sarcastically. Good Luck, Joaquin." "Take care," I said. I hung up the phone and from the corner of my eye noticed that Mike lowered the blinds to the window of his office. Finally, some privacy. About ten minutes later, he emerged. "Dude, I'm heading to a meeting. I will be back in an hour. Email me my messages." The day was almost over.

CHAPTER 6

TWO MONTHS LATER

I arrived in the office the Tuesday after Labor Day feeling good about my new job. It was still just a job not a career, but I was making decent money and saving it at the same time. I hadn't been on any auditions because my job had taken my focus away, and things had been slow with my acting anyway. For now, my role would be that of "assistant." Brenda would be back in a week and the weight of Mike breathing down my neck would finally subside. "This FedEx is for Mike Boo." Aisha handed me the envelope and nearly scratched me with her nails. Today, she reminded me of Mo'Nique with her hairstyle and tight clothing hugging every curve and love handle on her body living the mantra "big is beautiful." I walked through the corridor and all of the testers were planted in their chairs. Most of them were wearing the same clothes from the previous day. Their zombie-like movements were emphasized by their exhausted raccoon eyes. Mike hadn't walked in yet, but in anticipation of his arrival I grabbed his alkaline bottled water from the fridge and kept it on top of my desk. I looked at the FedEx envelope Aisha handed me and realized it was from famed Hollywood agent

Jack Goldstein. He was "the agent" in Hollywood. Netflix was rumored to be doing a show inspired by him. I was curious what was inside, but it had to wait until Mike arrived.

It was a quiet morning, because of this, I decided to browse for castings online. There was a small television near Brenda's desk that monitored the entrance to the office and the freight elevator entrance area. All of a sudden, I noticed Mike on the camera as he walked in through the office door, which swung open, and he shattered the glass again after intentionally banging the door against the wall. He then banged it a few more times taking out his anger on it. Another thing to add to my "to do" list today. Have the door repaired. "Oh Lawd," Aisha said. As he walked by I handed him his water. He grabbed it and flung it across the office, shattering two light fixtures. Mike unapologetically stormed into his office. "Joaquin, here, take her." By her, he was referring to his dog Regan. A spoiled English Bulldog, named after Linda Blair's character in The Exorcist. I hadn't met her yet because she spent the last two months in obedience school. She pranced around as if everyone was beneath her, but she was extremely friendly, the opposite of Mike. He purchased the dog when he was with an ex-girlfriend and the dog stayed longer than she did. He tried to unload her on his ex but even she didn't want the stubborn bitch. I grabbed Regan by the pink leash and immediately knew that the second he gave me cash, I would be off to a pet store to purchase a black or camouflage leash.

He still gave no indication as to why he was so upset. I hadn't done anything wrong, so maybe this was another tantrum screaming for attention since he lived alone and hated being single. He sat at his computer and remained frozen there with the most pissed-off face imaginable. I made sure to close out my Internet search when I realized I had an email from Brenda. I attempted to shield the screen just in case Mike decided to look over my shoulder.

Joaquin, I just wanted to let you know that I am not coming back to Imperial. My bastard husband scored a record deal and decided to leave me for a young blonde groupie he met while doing one of his shows in Hollywood. My nanny is taking care of my baby while I head to Miraval on my husband's credit card. If that asshole thinks he is getting away with making millions and leaving me with nothing, he is on crack. Anyway, I am sorry to leave you after you started working for Mike for such a short time. Good luck with him, you are going to need it. It's going to be an interesting adventure. If you feel like you get to the point where you are going crazy, open the bottom filing cabinet and look in the back. There you will have everything you need. I kept a few personal things under my desk so if you could please send those to my home, that would be great. Good luck and I wish you the best. Brenda

Now I had the distinct responsibility of being a zookeeper. I turned around and Mike was still staring at his computer screen. If I knew Brenda, she would have sent him a similar email. I finally looked in the back of the filing cabinet to see what Brenda kept stashed away. Inside, I found a Tiffany box the size of a cigar box. I knew she didn't leave any jewelry behind. I opened the box and inside I was welcomed by a meticulously organized pharmaceutical candy store that included Valium, Xanax, Adderall, edibles, injectable vitamins with brand new syringes, Ecstasy, a few bags of weed and four vials of Cocaine. Maybe Brenda should have gone to rehab, again, instead of Miraval.

"Joaquin, come here and bring your laptop," he yelled. I walked in and closed the door behind me. I realized that I couldn't hear anything outside of his office. The usual sounds of police sirens from the testers playing the video games couldn't be heard. I never noticed it before because Mike kept his door open so often to keep an ear on what was going on in the office. Mike noticed me taking in my new discovery. "My office is soundproofed; I don't need anyone to hear me when I don't want them to." I handed him the FedEx from Jack Goldstein and he grabbed it without looking at it and threw it behind the sofa. "Have a seat," he said. I attempted to sit on one of his chairs but first had to remove a pile of papers that were resting on top of it. "Be careful. Don't mess anything up." I didn't understand how I could possibly do that. To say his office was cluttered was an understatement. He and Rachael were pack rats, the only thing they had in common. As he began speaking, Rachael knocked on the door and entered his office. "What do you want?" Mike said. "I need to go over a couple of things with you regarding plot changes." "Not now. And nothing gets changed unless I want it to. Don't forget that!" Mike snapped. Rachael walked out of the office, closed the door, her face showed she was angered and felt rejected by her brother, yet again. Everyone in the office heard Mike rip into her. Although they were siblings, they didn't seem to be very close. It appeared that business came first then family, but for Mike it was more like business first, then me, myself, and I. "Brenda has chosen to leave the family. That traitor bitch is definitely blacklisted. This means, I would expect you to take on the role of my personal assistant. My life is in your hands. You have proven yourself in a short time and will have to continue to prove yourself to reassure me that I have made the right decision in giving you this responsibility. You will be paid more money, but along with that comes a great deal of work. My life becomes your life, my concerns become yours, and my hunger becomes your problem. Do you understand?" "Yes. I'm curious how much money will I be making now? I asked. "Right now, you are making $75,000 a year. I'm going to double it to $150,000." I was excited about the money, but at the same time knew that my life would be intensified a thousand times over. "The job will now require you to be available twenty-four-seven. I know when Brenda was here, you both left at 6:00 p.m. That no longer exists. If I need anything at any hour of the day or night, you will now be in charge of that." I kept my mind on the money and realized that I would have no life, which meant I would have to say goodbye to my acting aspirations, for now. Goodbye auditions. Was I selling out? At the moment, I didn't care. I was done with being a starving artist. I could always pursue acting later.

"I'm going away to Tokyo next week. I will need you to take care of the following things when I am gone. Brenda was supposed to, but now she doesn't exist. Make sure to get all of this. One, I want you to confirm my travel arrangements to Tokyo which should be squared away. I will be gone for one week and will be checking in with you periodically. You will need to contact Judith, our travel agent, and make sure that cunt booked my window seat. I want 4A. It's First Class, of course, and I always request the same seat. Tell her if she can't get it done, we won't need her business anymore." He looked over at me. "Two, I will need you to shred all of the files that I keep in the closet over there." He pointed to a closet door in his office that I hadn't noticed before. "Shred everything. The manual you have will instruct you on how to shred my documents." "Instructions on how to shred?" I asked with a puzzled look on my face. "Obviously you haven't read the manual. Make that number three. Read the fucking manual and memorize it so I don't have to tell you how to do your fucking job. Four, I will need these five DVDs purchased so they are here when I return. Although no one buys DVDs anymore, Mike still did. I scanned the list which he had written on a crumpled Post-it. Five, I will need all three of my cats taken to the vet. They are difficult to catch especially when they know they are being taken there. Take Regan as well, she is due for a checkup. Six, you see how my office looks now?" "I don't want it looking like this when I get back. I want it completely organized. That should be all for now." "Ok, I will take care of it."

I walked out of his office and could hear the sounds of gunshots and screams from the new Homicide game. The soundtrack of the office. Just Another day at Imperial. "Leave the door open," he said. I walked over to what was now officially my desk. I thought about all the tasks I needed to get done. The phone rang and I looked at the Caller ID and recognized it as Brenda. I picked up the phone. "Hello," I said. Mike quickly interrupted, "Is that Brenda?" He picked up the phone before I had the opportunity to respond. "Hang up," he shouted at me. I am sure she called to remind me about something else she might have forgotten to mention. "How could you do this to me, after all I have done for you, you fucking bitch. What the hell am I supposed to do?!" He slammed the phone and pulled it out of the socket and smashed it against the wall. This was my cue. I did remember seeing the part of the manual that mentioned that he had a habit of destroying his phones and that spare phones were kept in abundance in the storage cabinet. They were custom Polycom phones in high-gloss red. I brought the new phone into his office. He didn't even acknowledge that I was in his presence as he remained stone cold. I hooked up the phone and left his office with the broken phone. When I walked back to my desk, I noticed my voicemail notification was blinking. I found this odd because my phone didn't ring except for when Brenda called on Mike's line. I checked my voicemail hoping that I wouldn't be in store for more surprises. You have one new message: "Joaquin, this is Eric with Executive Travel. Judith had to leave today due to a family emergency. I am calling to confirm Mike's flight for Tuesday. Please call me, I would like to go over the details."

Unbelievable, they screwed up his departure date. I called Eric in hopes that Mike wouldn't hear the conversation. "Hi, Eric, it's Joaquin at Imperial. I received your message but found it weird that the flight is scheduled for Tuesday. Mike is supposed to leave on Monday evening." "I have him leaving on Tuesday. Judith had an emergency, and this is what I have in her notes as his itinerary," he said with an attitude. "Hold on one second." I tried to remain patient and professional. I decided to confirm with Mike what his exact plans were. I placed the phone down and walked into his office. "Mike, I am squaring things away for your trip and would like to confirm that you are leaving Monday evening, correct?" "Yes, make sure that cunt gets my seat." I rushed back to the phone. "Eric, I just spoke to Mike and he is supposed to depart on Monday." "Well, he is scheduled for Tuesday and everything is sold out and there is no way I can get him on that flight." I lost my patience with him and couldn't hold myself back. I tried to be as quiet as possible. "Don't be an asshole. Make sure to get him on that flight or you guys will lose us as a client and from what I understand, we are your biggest account so you can't afford to lose us. Not to mention, I am sure Judith wouldn't be pleased that you lost her biggest account on the one day she wasn't in the office." Eric remained silent. "I'll see what I can do. I will call you back in five minutes." "Make it happen and I will send you a PS4 console with a few of our games, T-shirts and sweatshirts." I hung up the phone. I knew that Eric was a twenty-something travel coordinator for Judith and was a big gamer. Mike kept video game consoles in his storage closet for moments like these. In the manual it stated that some of the video game consoles, games and promotional giveaways in the closet were for emergency bribery purposes. There was a note in the manual stating that anyone could be bought. I wanted to make sure that Mike got on that flight. The phone rang and I quickly picked it up, not giving Mike any indication that I was under a stressful situation. I knew the call was from Eric. "Hi Eric." "Hi, everything is taken care of. I had to bribe someone at Singapore Airlines who made it happen, so make that two PS4 systems. I have him going out on Monday night with his usual seat as requested." "Thank you. I'll send those out today." "Awesome, thanks and I am sorry about the inconvenience."

I hung up the phone and knew Mike was going to be gone for the next week and things in the office would be a lot calmer. I sat back in my chair and knew I had just avoided a crisis. Mike stepped out of his office and was off to a personal training session. I quickly gathered the systems, games and T-shirts from his closet and sent them via messenger to Eric. "Mission Accomplished."

CHAPTER 7

SEX, DRUGS & EAST L.A.

Today was a quiet day. Especially with Mike in Tokyo. Everyone could finally breathe. Workers had smiles on their faces and people were having non-work-related conversations. I decided to tackle all of the tasks he asked me to take care of. I began with shredding documents. I entered his office with a key that I finally had a copy of. Once inside, it was pure chaos. The mood definitely reflected his personality. I was overwhelmed by all the clutter. I avoided it for the moment and went straight for the closet that contained the files that he wanted me to shred. I turned the handle, but the door was locked. I checked his desk where he normally kept the copy of his house keys for Ana. I found an enormous round keychain that contained about a hundred keys, none of them labeled. I stood there trying to figure out which one opened the door, and it took me forty-five minutes to find the right one.

I opened the closet and couldn't believe my eyes. I was expecting a pile of boxes in a small closet, but I was now in a room with several shelves on both sides of me with file boxes, filled with papers that he wanted me to shred. He wanted the closet completely emptied because his trainer also practiced feng shui and told him that decluttering was vital to living a balanced life. I immediately started grabbing files from one of the boxes and began shredding the contents with a shredder he had in his office.

Halfway through the first box, I remembered that he had specific instructions for this process. I went to my desk to look at his bible to see how he wanted this mundane task done. *Shred all documents. Once contents are shredded make sure the bag is taken to my house and burned in the fireplace.* His paranoia reeked through the instructions. It took me three days to complete the entire closet. Towards the end of the third day, I came across several documents that caught my eye. They were in the last box that had a Post-it on it from Mike to Brenda instructing her to make sure to destroy the contents immediately. Of all of the boxes it was the only one labeled confidential in bold red. It was dated six months ago. Brenda obviously ignored him and threw the box to the back of the closet, out of sight. One of the documents stated the bonuses that were given to executives, producers, and testers in December of the previous year. I decided to hold onto that document for reference. The next documents were in a file labeled *Red Alert: 911*.

When I opened the folder, there were several screenshots of the animated character from the *Homicide* game engaging in an orgy with multiple female characters in a bedroom. The images showed the characters in various sexual positions and would allow the player to unlock these special areas of the game. The pages were marked "highly confidential" and only had Mike's name on it along with Raul Perez, who was the President of Imperial Latin America. He was based in Miami but covered all of Latin America to fill the market with Imperial's violent brand. It was extremely successful globally, but the Latin American market had a penchant for the violence and drugs in the game. I immediately realized why Mike wanted Brenda to destroy the files. She was probably so wrapped up with marriage drama that she let it slip through the cracks. I grabbed the file and kept that for my records as well.

Although *Homicide* was the most controversial game on the market, essentially this was porn. Up until that point, all of the documents I had been shredding were just a waste of paper and several game proposals fans sent Mike, hoping their idea would become the next big thing. Little did they know, they were all blatantly ignored and destroyed. I was at the office until 10:00 p.m. but was able to have the entire closet cleared out. This worked out perfectly because I still had Thursday and Friday to complete the rest of his assigned tasks. I decided to ask Lupita if she would clean and organize his office. She was an expert at organizing and I would pay her extra to do it. "Lupita, puedes hacer me el favor de limpiar y organizar la oficina de Mike?" "Ok mijo, no problem," she said. "Te voy a pagar extra." "No es necesario." "Si, te voy a pagar." "Ok, está bien." The next day, I grabbed Mike's keys and headed to his house and made sure to have all six, thirty-gallon trash bags in my car containing all of the documents I shredded. I had to be quick because the cats' appointment was for 2:30 p.m. and it was now 1:00 p.m. I knew it wasn't going to be easy rounding them up and I had to contend with traffic. I arrived at the gate and an older woman walking a Shih Tzu approached my car. "Excuse me?" she asked. "Are you the landscaper or the pool boy?" "I'm neither, I'm the personal assistant." "Oh, I just assumed anyone who drives a Prius must be in the service industry." "Is there a point to this conversation? Because I have work to do." "Tell your boss that the tree in the backyard needs to be trimmed. It's encroaching onto my property despite the fencing and hedges. Also, he needs to keep the noise level down, his music is too loud." "I'll be sure to let him know, have a good day."

I drove in and closed the gate behind me. I walked into Mike's house and was immediately accosted by Regan. She begged for my attention. I ignored her and looked for the cats. Two of them were comfortably planted on the sofa and the other was on the kitchen counter. Mike had all of them declawed to spare his furniture, so I knew I didn't have to worry about getting scratched. I looked in his utility closet for the three travel crates. The second I pulled them out and placed them on the floor, I turned around and all three cats had disappeared. I heard a cabinet door close and that was a clue I needed in order to find one of them. Other than that, I relied on Regan literally leading me to each of the cats' locations as if to rat them out because she thought she was going to have the place to herself. She led me straight to the kitchen and began barking at the top cabinets. I opened the cabinet door and there was Freddy. A large, black grizzly cat who immediately hissed at me. I opened it again and kept opening it and closing it to see if he would hiss each time and like a synchronized jack in the box, he hissed every single time. Finally, I closed the door and figured I would save him for last. I looked for Jason and Michael. He named all of the cats after the characters in his favorite horror films. Jason Vorhees, Freddy Krueger and Michael Myers. I found Jason under the bed and Michael deep in the closet resting on a pile of T-shirts. I decided they weren't worth my energy so I looked for cat food or anything that would get them to come out. I found three cans of solid white albacore tuna and the second I pulled them out of the pantry, all three cats emerged immediately. I didn't even bother putting the food on a plate; I opened each can and set them on the kitchen counter. Each of the cats were distracted with their own can so one by one I grabbed their cans and placed them inside each of the carriers that I had set on the floor with each of the doors opened. As planned, each of them went inside their carriers without a hitch.

I called Marek to pick me up so I wouldn't have to deal with parking while managing the cats. Marek arrived at the gate and I buzzed him in. I watched him on the monitor in the kitchen. Once he pulled up to the door, I grabbed two of the crates and placed them out front and went back to retrieve the third. I could hear them devouring the tuna. I grabbed Regan and got into the SUV. The cats began to cry, sounding like young children. They knew they were headed to the vet and were not happy. We began to pull out and of course with my luck, Mike's cheerful neighbor was about to cross with her dog and husband in tow. She signaled us to pass, and Marek continued to drive slowly. She knocked on the passenger window. I rolled it down. "Hello," I said as the cats continued to cry. Her dog began to growl, Regan began to bark and each of the cats began to hiss. Her dog was frightened and began to whine. "What is that awful sound?" "It's your voice," I said. "You really should learn how to control those fleabags, ugh. There, there, Chloe. They are stressing out my poor Chloe," she said as she picked up her dog. I looked at her husband. "You really should learn to control your bitch. Your dog could use some manners as well," I said as I put my sunglasses on. I noticed her dog began to take a dump out of nervousness all over the woman's Chanel tweed jacket. "Oh, and by the way, your dog just took a shit on your jacket. That is just unacceptable, unless you are into that sort of thing." "She's definitely not," her husband said as he chuckled. She hit him in the gut, and I rolled up the window. "Let's go, Marek." We began our journey to their vet's office in West Hollywood. In the meantime, I took the time to begin hunting down the DVDs he requested on my phone. I decided to try Amoeba, Cinephile, and Rockaway Records. I was able to locate two of the DVDs. Somehow, I knew it wasn't a coincidence when the clerk at Amoeba responded with "Yeah, good luck finding those."

Once I arrived at the vet's office, the cats were screaming for their lives as if someone was pulling the fur off their bodies with tweezers. The vet saw me immediately because the cats were causing a ruckus with the dogs in the waiting room. Everything was peaceful until I walked in with three spoiled Hancock Park cats. After the cats and Regan received their check-ups and clean bills of health, I packed them up and rushed back to Mike's place. I burned all of the shredded documents as Mike requested, which took me two hours. I decided to take Regan for a walk before taking her back to the office since she had to stay with me. I continued to call every video and music store. Even Amazon had people selling the films for $300 a piece, used, because the new ones were impossible to obtain. I returned to the office and sat on my chair frustrated, trying to figure out what my next move was. I stared at my screen and could now relate to the other workers as they sat with their motionless gaze. I looked up and there was an attractive guy who I hadn't met or seen before. He had chestnut brown hair perfectly coiffed, scruffy facial hair and chic style. Right away, he seemed to know what I was doing. "You can't find the DVDs, can you?" "How did you know what I was looking for?" "I am Gavin Kent, the VP of Production. I work closely with Mike and I just returned from San Francisco." "Hi, how are you? I'm Joaquin." "Yes, I know, I've heard a lot about you." "Good, I hope." "It doesn't matter whether it was good or bad, what matters is that I heard about you. I believe these are what you are looking for." He handed me the DVDs I had been searching for. "How did you know I was looking for these?" "It's a test Mike always gives to his assistants. He actually already owns the films, but he wants to see if you can get them. He is setting you up to fail because the DVDs are discontinued, and you have to pay a fortune for used or bad copies in order to obtain them. I, on the other hand, own several copies of each because we used it for research for a game several years ago." "So why are you helping me?" "When you work closely with Mike, it's good to help each other out. Today, only you are under a microscope but on any given day, we all are. The floors are covered with eggshells here. Everyone has their day when he places a gun to your head. I usually don't help his assistants out. So far only you and Brenda. Her because she has big tits and you because Mike seems to like you. He will be impressed that you got them and then he will throw them aside and forget all about them and give you another test." "Thanks for the heads up."

Gavin went into his office, grabbed his Saint Laurent leather jacket, and left the office. I looked at the DVDs on my desk and realized that my tasks were almost completed. I had his films, the cats and Regan went to the vet, I paid Lupita to clean his office, and I shredded all of his documents. It was Friday and I relaxed in my chair knowing that the weekend should be a calm one after such a hectic work week. The phone rang, it was Mike. "I need you to call that number in the manual and make arrangements for Shana to be at my place at 10:00 p.m. Also, I need you to go to East L.A.; Marek will know where to take you. There's a blue envelope in my desk drawer, it contains $500. You are going to meet Romalice, give him the envelope and he will give you a package for me. Take the package to my house along with a list of groceries I am going to email to you. Make sure everything is organized and don't screw anything up. In my filing cabinet, there are cans of mace and brass knuckles. They were promo items from our game Looters. Take them with you just in case." "Ok, I'll take care of everything." He hung up. In the span of one minute, my Friday night disappeared. Instead of having a drink, I was headed to a pit-bull infested warzone. I looked in Mike's office to make sure everything was straightened up so it was ready when he arrived on Monday. I checked my phone for his email with the grocery list.

Subject: Groceries

From Whole Foods:

loads of dark chocolate

organic beef burgers

carton of eggs

Irish cheddar

Quest Protein Bars

raw cashews

alkaline water

green tea

canned garbanzo beans

six cans of ginger beer

four cans of lentil soup

organic flax seeds

fresh watermelon

Asian pears

organic whole milk

strawberries

whipped cream

Ben & Jerry's Cherry Garcia

From CVS: Trojan Condoms and Preparation H Hemorrhoid Cream

From Jo Malone: buy a large Pomegranate Noir candle

From John Kelly Chocolates: one Signature Chocolate Tower

I looked at the list and assumed Mike was going to binge all weekend. I noticed it was 3:00 p.m. and I had to accomplish all of these things and return to Mike's place by 8:00 p.m. I called Marek immediately. "Joaquin, what's up?" he asked. "I have to run errands for Mike before he arrives, can you please come back to the office?" "Sure, no problem. I'm ten minutes away." I walked out of the office building and into the SUV.

"Marek, our first stop will be Romalice's place in East L.A." "Fuck." He shakes his head. "I'm guessing you have been there many times before." "Yes, always on Fridays with Brenda." He accelerated in annoyance. "I'm sure it's not your favorite place to drive to." "No, not at all. It's a rough area. A lot of gang and police activity. The last time I took Brenda there, a few gangbangers offered her money for a lay. She was pissed when the guys kept saying, 'twenty dollars for a lay baby.' She screamed at them that her pussy was like shopping at Fred Segal and that their ghetto asses couldn't afford it." "Really?" I laughed, "Then what happened?" "They pulled out their guns, she screamed, ran into my SUV and we got the fuck out of there. I am driving you there, but I don't know what you are doing, and I don't want to know." "Marek, I don't exactly know what I am doing there other than picking something up." "I don't need to know anymore," he said with a smirk in the mirror. It was still early so we were moving rather quickly for L.A. standards.

We were entering East L.A. Gone were the DTLA hipsters and skyscrapers. For a second it felt as though we traveled to a Third World war zone where the residents were neglected and forgotten because they were so disconnected from the rest of the population. East L.A. was not pretty. Not that downtown was stunning, but I was expecting to see Anderson Cooper on a corner broadcasting from the frontlines. Guns were alarm clocks and instead of a view of the Hollywood sign, you had a view of a juvenile correctional facility for delinquents. We arrived at Romalice's address. From the outside, it appeared to be a crack den disguised as an apartment building. I couldn't imagine that people actually lived in the structure. "Make sure you are out in ten minutes. I don't like to be parked with the Escalade here for long because it draws too much attention from the gangbangers and the cops." "Trust me, I don't intend on staying here long."

I walked into the building and looked at all of the buzzers. I buzzed number twenty-two. "Who is it?" a voice shouted through the intercom. "I'm Mike's Assistant," I said. "Where's Brenda?" The suspicion could be heard in his voice. "She no longer works for Mike." The door buzzed and I pushed the door as my hand stuck to it because of some sticky residue. I was immediately grossed out. As I entered the building, I was welcomed by the stench of urine. I reached a fork in the ghetto road. I had to decide whether or not to take the run-down elevator or the poorly lit stairs. I opted for the stairs to avoid being confined in a rickety tin box. I walked up the stairs to the second floor and the large numbers on the doors read 5, 6, and 7. Each flight I completed, I could hear a distinct soundtrack to each floor. The third floor was a couple arguing about money, the fourth floor was a woman screaming at one of her kids in Spanish, and the fifth floor was a couple having sex. When I arrived on the sixth floor, I noticed it was eerily silent in comparison to the others. I looked down the hall and realized that a lot of the lights were out and there was yellow police tape adorning the doors to several of the apartments.

I arrived at my destination, which was the 7th and top floor. I immediately spotted number twenty-two and knocked on the door. At the same time, I received a text message on my cell from Marek. *Hurry up boss.* I heard someone removing several chains and locks from the door. The door opened slowly and there stood a muscular Latino guy in a wife beater with several tattoos on his arms, neck and face. "You got the money?" he asked. "Yes." "Come in, homie." I entered the apartment while handing him the envelope. He proceeded to count the money in it. I was distracted because I was looking around the apartment and was astonished at how expensively decorated it was. I got a brief glimpse of the kitchen which had stainless steel Viking appliances and the living room walls weren't plastered with posters of *Scarface*. Instead, they were black and white photographs tastefully done. I couldn't imagine he convinced a decorator to come to East L.A. to do the work. I turned to my right and noticed four dog crates with pit-bulls in each one of them. All four seemed to be barking but not a sound could be heard from them. Martha Stewart's Chow Chows they were not. "Why aren't they making any noise?" I asked. "I'm counting my money, don't interrupt me." Once he was finished counting, he handed me a small bag and explained the silent dogs. "Because, I had their voice boxes removed just in case anybody tries to break into my crib, they won't know that there are four dogs in here until they get attacked."

On that note, I was ready to leave. Regan didn't know how good she had it. "Cool," I said, although I was horrified at the fact he would do that to the dogs, but I didn't have time to care. I had to go so I opened his door and stepped out. "Thanks," I said. I began walking down the stairwell when I received another text from Marek. *COPS! Meet me at the corner!* All of a sudden, I could see movement up the stairwell. I probably had just purchased a great deal of narcotics and the last thing I needed was to be stopped by them. I ran back to Romalice's apartment and thankfully he hadn't locked the door when I walked out. "The cops are coming up the stairs." Romalice began pulling out a variety of weapons. All four dogs were aggressively barking silent barks. I needed to act quickly. I jumped on top of one of the crates and the one dog was trying to bite me through it. "I'm going to let the dogs out, hide in the ceiling vent," Romalice said. I jumped up, removed the cover, and pulled myself up. As I was closing the cover, Romalice released all four dogs and opened the apartment door to release the hellish hounds. He quickly closed it. The dogs sprinted out like soldiers. I could hear an officer yelling because one of the dogs had attacked him and followed by gunshots, presumably killing them. "Open up! Police!" I heard one of the officers shout. "Fuck you!" Romalice shouted. It sounded as though they were going to bust Romalice.

I began moving through the ceiling vent but could hear what was going on. I heard the door being smashed and several gunshots followed by a moment of silence. "We got him!" the officer yelled. "I thought I heard another voice in the apartment," another officer said. "The coast is clear." I continued going through the ceiling vent, hoping it would lead somewhere, until I realized I was above the trash room on the same floor. I jumped down and stayed there for a few minutes. I placed the package in my pants and walked out of the trash room. Officers were inside of the apartment, but I was further down the hall. I made my way down a different stairwell and made it to the ground level.

I walked out of the building and there was a lot of commotion. People who lived in the building were outside. I blended with the crowd out front and as I made my way towards the corner, I bumped into a nicely dressed man. "Excuse me, sorry," I said. "Hey." "Yes?" I said as I turned around. "Do you live here?" He asked. I immediately thought he could tell I didn't belong there. I had to use my acting skills in order to get myself out of this. "No officer." "What's your name? And what are you doing here?" "My name is Jose and I'm visiting my Aunt and my cousins on da fifth floor. I haven't seen dem in a while." "I'm Detective Rivera. Have you seen anything suspicious going on?" "No, nothing, unless you consider my aunt smackin' my cousins for breakin' her remote during her novela suspicious, it's been quiet from what I've seen." I was dying to get back to Marek as I kept the package under my shirt. "Ok, well as I said, my name is Detective Rivera. If you see any suspicious activity or if your aunt does, you give me a call. Here is my card." "Okay, will do detective, have a great day," I said. I continued walking to the corner and turned left where I saw Marek waiting. I jumped into the Escalade. "About fucking time boss," Marek said. We sped off. "What took you so long? Once I saw the cops, I moved immediately. I drove the fuck around and this is the hood, it's not scenic. "Cops raided Romalice's apartment." "I don't want to know anymore. Don't tell me anything." Marek was paid to drive and be blind to everything Mike exposed him to. "Marek let's stop by Mike's house next. I want to drop off this package." "You got it boss."

He drove me to Mike's house, and I dropped off the package. I left it in the drawer of his nightstand. I then rushed out to complete the grocery shopping. On our way to Whole Foods, I decided to call Shana to confirm for the evening. The phone rang and a woman answered the line. "Client's last name?" she asked in a sultry voice. "Chapman," I said. "Shana will be at the agreed destination at 10:00 p.m." "Okay, sounds good." I said. She hung up. Easy enough, I had that task off of my list. Marek proceeded to Whole Foods, which was predictably a madhouse. I picked up his condoms and hemorrhoid cream at CVS. By the time we reached the last two stops, which were Nordstrom at The Grove for the Jo Malone candle and John Kelly Chocolates in Hollywood, I was exhausted. I was cutting it close on time since I knew Mike's flight was getting in soon.

Just before we arrived back at Mike's place, Marek received a flight alert on his phone. "Joaquin, bad news, Mike's flight is delayed by an hour." This was good in the sense that I had more time to prepare, but bad because Mike will be in a terrible mood. Hopefully Shana could change that, I didn't want to think about how. I grabbed all the bags and headed into the house. With his flight delayed, this meant I was going to meet Shana, which definitely wasn't part of Mike's plan. I called Shana's number to see if she could reschedule but apparently she was booked solid after Mike. Mike only had her for a couple of hours. Either Mike was cheap, not impressive in bed or she was so in demand. I was curious to see what she looked like. Once all of the groceries were put away, I lit the candles so the air could mask the remnants of marijuana that was still lingering from Mike's last smoke session. I placed his Preparation H under the bathroom sink behind everything so Shana wouldn't discover it. I finished prepping and sat on his sofa and relaxed as I stared at the ceiling thinking to myself that I had accomplished everything. It felt good and at the same time I couldn't believe it was a Friday night and I was making sure everything was perfect at my boss's place so he could get laid. I closed my eyes and began to fall asleep.

****

I woke up and heard the doorbell ring. It was weird, I hadn't heard anyone buzz from the gate. "Who is it?" I asked. There wasn't a reply. I opened the door, and everything was pitch black. I couldn't see anything. I heard the click of a gun and the flash of shots going off.

****

I woke up startled by the dream. The buzzer to the gate was ringing. I picked up the receiver. "Hello," I said. "It's Shana." She sounded like a phone sex operator. "Ok, buzzing you in now." She drove in and parked her Mercedes. Shana emerged, she had long blonde hair, oversized breasts hugged by a double-breasted Prada jacket and black Jimmy Choo boots. "Hello, Shana, I'm Joaquin, Mike's new assistant." I said. "Hi Joaquin, nice to meet you." We entered the house. "Can I take your jacket for you?" "No, I'm naked underneath, but thank you." "Would you like something to drink?" "Sure, wine would be great." "Red or white?" "White." I reached for a bottle of Sancerre from the wine fridge. I poured her a glass and handed it to her. She grabbed the glass, walked over to the sofa and sat down making herself comfortable as if she were in her own home.

"Mike's flight was delayed so he should be here soon." "How long have you been working for Mike?" "Not long at all," I said. "And how do you like it so far?" "It's a job and I make good money, it works for now." "Working for Mike doesn't seem like a job, it seems like a curse. He has so much anger inside of him," she said. "Yeah, he's definitely pissed at the world and I don't understand why. He has everything." "Having sex with him sometimes feels like he just wants to rip me apart. He definitely has a lot going on in his head, but I don't give a shit. I just hand him my body and he is one of my top clients," she said. "That's a graphic description." "There is nothing subtle about this business, especially when you are dealing with high-powered men. Everything is straightforward. Which is the way I like it. Emotions are checked at the door." "Do you believe in love?" I asked. "I love myself and I love money. The people, who follow their hearts, end up poor, broken-hearted, divorced, and/or forever linked because they decided to have children. I don't believe in monogamy, so I cater to several wealthy men, which in turn keeps me wealthy and in control." "The art of being cold," I said. "Exactly, you have to be a monster to get what you want. Your job working for Mike is perfect because he is going to make you a monster, if he hasn't already, and he would be the one who would have to watch out," she winked. I smiled as I drank my wine and she polished off her glass. "I've always dreamt of being an actor, not necessarily a monster." "Baby, Hollywood is filled with monsters, I've slept with plenty of them. Consider your job bootcamp, remember I said that." "Would you like another glass of wine?" "No, I have to be awake and energized when he arrives." My phone began to ring. It was Mike. "Is Shana there?" "Yes, she is here." "Did you purchase everything I asked for? Is everything squared away?" "Yes, everything is taken care of." "Good, come outside to collect my bags, I am five blocks away." "Will do." I hung up and turned to Shana. "He is five blocks away." "I enjoyed your company and conversation. We'll have to do it again sometime." "Sure thing," I said. "I hope to see you on TV at the Academy Awards someday," she said as she headed to the bathroom to freshen up. "Me too, me too." I walked out.

As I exited the house, the black Escalade pulled up and stopped right in front of me as Mike emerged from the vehicle. "That was a fucking disaster. If I could blame that bitch Judith for my delay, I definitely would." I didn't say a word, I let him vent and just stared at him as he ranted, and I began to tune him out. His mouth was moving but I didn't hear a thing. I knew everything was a complaint and how someone didn't take care of him the way he expected them to. As Mike's "woe is me" speech continued, Marek began unloading his ten pieces of Tumi luggage. "I may have you come with me on my next trip to make sure everything runs a lot better, and I don't have to deal with the population." That part I did hear as all of a sudden, the thought of traveling around the world was exciting, yet I knew I wouldn't see much of the destination when I would be there to make sure he had a smile on his face which was definitely impossible to accomplish. I quickly changed the subject. "Shana is inside waiting for you." "Great, take the bags upstairs and then you can go."

He began to enter the house as Marek helped me to take the bags inside. "Joaquin, I will be in the bedroom. Leave everything in one of the guest bedrooms, you can unpack everything tomorrow." "No problem." He proceeded to go up-stairs with Shana as I began placing bags in the foyer. Marek helped me with the rest. "Thanks, Marek, have a goodnight." "Goodnight, boss." As I continued to walk up the stairs, two pieces at a time, I could already hear Mike's grunting. Re-gan was planted outside the bedroom door, sniffing out the situation by the crevice under the door. I placed the bags in one of the guest rooms and noticed it was past midnight. My Friday night was gone. As I finished, I could hear Mike's grunting getting louder and louder and Shana was matching his sounds. I felt like I was on porn set. He was finally getting laid. I closed the door to his house and returned back to my life in Hollywood, the zip code, not the lifestyle. At least not yet.

CHAPTER 8

THE RESET BUTTON

I didn't hear from Mike all weekend, so I assumed things went well and there weren't any issues with his life. I walked into the office, Monday morning, thirty minutes early, and it was extremely quiet. I was one of the first employees in the office and it reminded me of the solace of a library which felt so peaceful. If only the rest of the day would have remained like that. I turned on my computer and looked at the calendar and realized that *Homicide III* was going to be released tomorrow. Mike got laid over the weekend and the new game was about to launch, which meant he should be in a great mood. At least for the first couple of hours.

I went onto GameSpot and IGN and they both gave *Homicide III* excellent reviews across the board. He was going to be thrilled. Moments later, he blasted through the office. "Water!" he shouted. I should have learned early on not to have high expectations. I grabbed his alkaline water and brought it to him. He walked into his immaculate office and didn't mention how great it looked or how organized it was. Something was definitely on his mind. "Make sure the conference room is free at 11:00 a.m.," he said. I walked out and couldn't understand why he was so angry. He was just being himself, but he was at the point of rage today. He obviously didn't care that the new game was getting great reviews and he was going to make a killing financially. He had greater problems.

When I returned to my desk, I wondered what it could be. I searched the Internet for headlines because I noticed that was what he was doing when I walked out of his office. Apparently, it was just announced that California Senator Kyle Walters was targeting Imperial because of the violence depicted in the games and he wanted to stop the sale of them, specifically to children. He felt that the games glorified crime, guns, gang activity, and drug cartels. In the climate we lived in, where school shootings had become so common, Imperial was number one on his hit-list because the company was notorious for releasing the most violent games and setting the industry standard for ultra-realistic nefarious entertainment. He wanted the games to have an adult rating, which would affect where they could be sold and affect sales on a global scale. He was being groomed for the next presidential race so this victory would appear great on his resume to the American public, especially parents. At a time when Mike should have been celebrating, now he had to regroup and figure out, along with his staff, how to handle this situation. He wanted me to sit in on the meeting and although I didn't know why, my guess was that he wanted me very close in case he got hungry, and he wanted me to fetch him food. I was interested in seeing the dynamics of how this particular sit-down would play out. He never had me sit it on these meetings before and this meeting was going to be attended by his closest confidants. I noticed it was 10:55 a.m. so I decided to set up for the meeting. I placed bottled water and an assortment of soft drinks on the table. Mike briefly walked in.

"What the fuck is this?" "What do you mean?" "Don't give them my water, get a pitcher from the kitchen and fill it with tap water and use paper cups." I scrambled and picked up the bottles of water and set everything up as he instructed. Charles Santos walked in and I could tell he was sweating. He knew he had his work cut out for him. We both sat down and shortly after, Rachael, August, Gavin, Christina and Mike walked in. Mike sat at the head of the table to display his authority. "As you have all heard, that fucking piece of shit Kyle Walters is trying to sabotage my fucking game and company because he thinks it is badly influencing the fucking youth in this country." He slammed his fist on the table and got louder. Everyone froze.

"It is not my fucking responsibility to make sure that children are raised properly. It is their parent's fucking job, and they are obviously the ones buying the games for them. I want this to go away. He is trying to change our rating from Mature to Adult, which means our games would be available in fewer stores." Everyone remained silent and continued to listen. I watched each person, who was normally a monster to their direct reports, squirming in their seats. No one wanted to be on the firing end of Mike's verbal ammunition. Each one of them appeared to age a few years in that short moment from the stress of the situation. Mike's life was wearing on them and I refused to be one of those people. He looked at each employee and explained how he wanted the situation handled and listened to each of their ideas. Although he listened, it seemed as though he wasn't there. He was already thinking about something else.

One hour later, we all emerged from the conference room looking exhausted. It was an emotional rollercoaster. Just as I was exiting the room, he pulled me aside. "J, did you shred everything in my closet as I requested?" Clearly, he hadn't bothered to check for himself. "Yes, I did, everything is gone." "Good." Something that stood out to me in the meeting was

Rachael's vibe when Mike spoke to her. It was obvious to me that Rachael was jealous of Mike, but it seemed more than the typical sibling rivalry. She tolerated him because Mike made her a millionaire, giving her the lifestyle but none of the glory. Rachael was always in Mike's shadow and Mike liked to remind her of that through his control and power over her.

Mike probably felt as though Rachael owed him and in turn Mike felt he owned his sister. Mike scooped Rachael up from a dismal career lull when Rachael left a stint at *Los Angeles Magazine* to trek the globe for a few years. She had no clue what she wanted to do with her life whereas Mike always did. Mike knew he wanted to make money and make video games. Rachael was only two years younger than Mike, but the only thing they had in common was their icy demeanor. Now Rachael took orders from her big brother and she envied the respect and accolades that Mike received for the company's achievements. This seemed like a deeply rooted issue from childhood. Rachael wanted to be feared by her employees as everyone feared Mike, so she treated everyone badly as well. However, there was an inter-office joke going around because Rachael was a writer and wrote most of the scripts for the games. During her travels she tried to become a novelist or memoirist, but she failed. She had hoped that her jaunt around the world would have manifested into a fictional manuscript or a find yourself memoir like *Eat, Pray, Love*. However, when she first started at Imperial, her writing was shit and slammed by the critics. So as the games evolved, no one knew she hired a ghostwriter for the games. However, as Chief Creative Officer, Rachael would get the name credit as the sole writer. It was her way of cheating to gain the attention and the accolade she craved. It was not enough. Mike was aware of this and since the *Homicide* games were his babies, he wanted the best writers. This was the bone he threw to Rachael. Although they were siblings, the bridge between them was burning slowly. The following day, *Homicide III* was released and set the record for the highest grossing video game ever. Mike was not only a president, mastermind and founder, he was on the verge of becoming a legend. He was changing the face of video games forever. At this point he couldn't care less what Kyle Walters was trying to do. He was smiling all the way to the bank.

CHAPTER 9

HAPPY BIRTHDAY

Mike enjoyed gossip. Especially if it didn't involve him. He was like a woman in that way and definitely liked to know about the personal lives of his employees during the short amount of time they were able to have a social life. These were the same employees who thought Mike liked them because he spoke to them in the hall over a recent film, music or video game. It could have been about anything and instantaneously they believed they were part of Mike's circle. It didn't take long for me to realize that unless you were willing to give all of your time to the company, you were not part of his inner circle. Even then, you weren't immune to his wrath. What saved me was that I knew too much about Mike's personal and professional life, and no one else did. What many people didn't know was that his bark was worse than his bite. Surprisingly, he hated confrontation, especially outside of the company. He had no problem yelling at people at Imperial but outside was a different story, and he preferred that I take care of his dirty work for him. Within the doors of Imperial, he felt powerful, outside he thought more about his actions.

The next few weeks would be cause for celebration. *Homicide III* was doing very well in sales, topping its predecessor. The controversy surrounding the game from Kyle Walter's onslaught only helped generate more sales. Everyone was thrilled but more importantly, Mike was happy. Raises and bonuses were on the horizon and so was Mike's annual birthday celebration which I was in charge of handling. From what I heard, with his previous birthday celebrations, Mike always pretended as though he didn't want a party. Christina and Brenda would caress his ego and tell him that he was too fabulous not to have one. His birthday parties were held at a different venue every year. Imperial would rent out an entire restaurant or bar to celebrate the occasion. This year, his birthday would take place in the Art's District at an arcade bar with a nostalgic vibe. Rachael's birthday was three days after Mike's, and I remember Brenda had mentioned to me that he scoffed at the idea of sharing his birthday celebration with Rachael when she suggested the party should be for the both of them. Mike wanted no part of it. He wanted the attention for himself and he said if his sister wanted to have a party for her birthday, then she can fucking pay for it. I had to make sure that everything was as grand as possible. Balloons had to blanket the ceiling as if clouds were descending upon us. His favorite color, blood red so all the balloons had to be custom made so they could be the exact shade. It was very reminiscent of *The Shining* as it looked as though blood was dripping from the ceiling, possibly foretelling the future. His cake was another custom order because it had to feed 150 people and was a gun with red velvet inside. There was unlimited food and booze for all the employees.

I arrived at the place early to make sure everything was on schedule and that they were prepared to receive all of the employees, eager to eat and more importantly drink.

There would be an eating contest, which was an annual occurrence, where several employees would enter to see who could eat the most insects, cow balls, scorpions, water bugs and anything else that could be seasoned and cooked. The prize was $1,000 cash. I wouldn't be surprised if they grabbed the large water bugs from the streets of skid row. They would scarf these interesting delicacies and each participant had a bucket to vomit in case any of them got sick. Most of them did. Historically, the winner of the contest was always the most overweight or unattractive person in the company. Either way, it was the one who you knew wasn't going to go home to anyone special. I enjoyed my first of Mike's birthday parties in which everything went well, and I definitely had my share of drinks. Everyone had a genuine smile on their face, even Mike, which was rare. However, this was the first time and as I would soon learn, the last time everyone would. Two weeks after the party, I was looking forward to getting my raise and bonus. Everyone around me seemed to be getting their employee reviews and walked out of their boss's offices with smiles. I awaited mine but didn't know when it was going to happen until Gavin Kent walked up to my desk and said that he needed to speak to me. "Joaquin, can you come into my office please?" he said. I followed him into his oversized cubicle and although there wasn't soundproofing installed; he closed the sliding door behind us to buffer some of the conversation. I could smell the cologne in the air as soon as I walked in. This time, it was L'Homme by Yves Saint Laurent perched on his desk. "I'm giving you your yearly review because Mike doesn't do praise." "What do you mean?" "I'm joking, but Mike doesn't enjoy this part of the business." "You mean the part that forces him to tell his employee what a good job he has done," I said with sarcasm. He smirked and I could tell he appreciated my humor. "Well, Mike prefers to show his appreciation through money. Which, quite frankly, is the language everyone speaks and I'm sure all you care about. Compliments mean nothing, tomorrow they can turn to insults, but money can fuel a smile much longer and not to mention make life better." "I won't disagree with you there." "I know he is very pleased with you but will not say it, which is why I am here talking to you. You will be getting a $25,000 raise and a $25,000 bonus."

My face lit up in excitement, but I wanted to maintain my composure, so it showed that I felt as though I knew I deserved that. "Thank you," I said. "You deserve it. Your birthday is coming up in a week. What would you like for your birthday? Mike wants to know what you want for your birthday." "I don't know," I mumbled, taken aback as the thought of Mike getting me a present never entered my mind. "Is there anything you need?" I decided to be ballsy, "I would love a MacBook Pro." "Ok, you got it. Christmas is coming up so you will have to let me know what you want then as well. Welcome to the family," he said. "Thanks…I think." I smiled, and he smiled and stood up. "Just remember the people that can hurt you the most are those closest to you. Families can be your greatest allies and even greater enemies. Always watch your back, man." "Why are you telling me this?" "We produce games where the characters are cut-throat, out for themselves, families' stab each other in the back, people are on a mission of being at the top and they don't care who they have to hurt in order to get there. Where do you think we get the inspiration for the games? It isn't pulled out of our asses or thin air." "Thanks for the advice." He pulled the sliding door open, and I stepped out and he closed it again. I just had my first official employee review and I felt like I was being initiated into a gang. A gang of white boys and I was the only Puerto Rican. It turned out that the closer I became to the "family," the more disconnected many employees became from me. I was no longer seen as a fellow employee; instead, I was seen as someone who was close to the president and no one wanted to be near me. I was his eyes and ears at the company and people soon began to take notice. I knew he was very fickle and had a hot and cold personality. He could like me one minute and despise me the next. I knew this personality very well because he was a Scorpio, the most intense sign of the Zodiac. However, it is also the most dangerous. Just like me.

CHAPTER 10

THE PHOTOSHOOT

Despite the fact that my acting career was on hold at the moment, I still indulged my need for attention through a great photoshoot. Sure, I could post selfies all day for likes and to create thirst traps but when a photographer stops you on the street and tells you he wants to take photos of you, you take a moment to listen to what he has to say. Especially if the photographer is hot. I was walking on Hollywood Boulevard coming back from an intense session at Barry's Bootcamp, when a guy with dark features, beard, and hazel eyes looked in my direction across the street. I noticed him but my eyes immediately went to the camera on his neck and tattoos blanketed both of his arms. He looked Mediterranean or Middle Eastern and it turns out he was Greek. I waited for the crosswalk to change and when it did, I began to cross as he stood there smiling at me. I smiled back.

"Hi, how are you?" "Hi, I'm great thanks, you?" "I'm good, exhausted, coming from the gym and walking home." "Where is home?" "Walking distance from here," I said as I laughed and so did he. "I noticed you from across the street and immediately knew that I wanted to take pictures of you." "What kind of pictures?" "Headshots, body shots, I was thinking of a variety. I'm sure you'll be able to use them because you have to be an actor." "No, not quite, aspiring actor yes, but right now my acting career is on hold." "We have to change that. You should come to my studio in DTLA. It's my loft but my studio is there as well." He handed me his business card. "Get in touch with me and you'll get some good shots out of it." "How much do you charge?" "Come over and we'll talk about that. I'm more interested in creating art. I don't like to talk about money." "In this town? I doubt that." "Ok, I'll be in touch, I said." "Good, I'll speak to you soon." As I walked away, he began snapping a few shots of me. "Just practicing." I walked away and what I really wanted to do was have sex with him in that very moment. Yes, I'm interested in the photos but damn, he looked like someone should be photographing him. I waited a few days to send him a text to hopefully schedule it.

Hi, Kostas, it's Joaquin. It was great meeting you earlier this week, I'm reaching out to see when you'd be free to shoot the photos. Let me know.

Hi, Joaquin, are you free to stop by this Saturday? If so, stop by at 2:00 p.m.

Ok, yes, that works for me.

Perfect, come to the address on the card I gave you and I'll see you then.

Sounds good, I'll see you on Saturday.

That Saturday, I headed to L.A.'s Arts District. He lived in the Toy Factory Lofts, which I was familiar with because I had an ex that lived there but thankfully moved back to New York. I buzzed his apartment number and he immediately buzzed me in. As I walked in, the elevators were already open, so I ran in and the doors closed. I arrived on his floor and walked towards his apartment, the door was already ajar. I pushed it open. "Hello." "Hi Joaquin, how are you?" "I'm fine thanks, how are you?" Although I didn't have to ask because I knew how he was. He was shirtless and in front of me with not six but eight pack abs. He walked over and hugged me. "Sorry, I'm putting a shirt on now." "Do what makes you comfortable," I said. "You can put your bag there and organize your clothes on that rack," he said. I placed all of my clothes on the rack, and he returned back from the studio area.

"Let's start with that," he said as he pointed to a tank top and jeans. "Sounds good." I took my clothes off and dropped them on the floor. I was naked and was fully comfortable and quickly got dressed. I walked out slowly to where he was setting up the camera and lights. "Stand in the center, I want to check the light." I stood there as the flashes went off and I tried to envision a future where I was an actor and I'd have photoshoots like this all of the time. "Let's get started." "Sorry, my mind was somewhere else for a second." We went through several series of shots and changes of clothes. Two hours had passed. "Did you bring swim trunks?" "Yes, I did." "Ok, put those on." I walked over to the changing area to change into my trunks and as I dropped my clothes on the floor, he appeared behind me. "Now, this is what I'm talking about." He began touching my back. I turned around and he was completely naked and fully erect. He went in for the kiss and I wasn't going to stop him. We ended up in the bedroom where he pushed me onto his crisp white sheets. "You don't have a boyfriend or girlfriend that's going to walk in on us, right?" "Does it matter?" "What's your HIV status?" "I'm a top. I'm negative," he said. "I'm negative and on PREP," I said. "Perfect." We continued to kiss until he aggressively held me down, kissed me and paused for a moment while he reached for the lube. He began lubing his penis and then my ass. He threw the bottle to the side and he slowly slid inside of me. We went through the alphabet of sexual positions until we both ejaculated and remained in the bed exhausted. A few moments later, he got up and looked at me. "You're fucking beautiful." I smiled. "Thanks, you are too." "I need to photograph you." I quickly became alert. "What? Not naked." "Yes naked, you look amazing, it's natural. They will be beautiful black and white photos. He quickly walked back into the bedroom and began taking several partially nude photos of me on the bed. "Now, some full nudes, I want you to express your vulnerability." He pulled the sheets off of me and I was completely naked. He took some shots where I was full frontal. I quickly jumped up. "Delete those." "No, it's art, sexy man." "No, please delete it." "Ok, I will."

He showed me that he did. I rested on his bed, but I knew our time was winding down and the moment where we said our goodbyes and "never see each other again" was approaching. I got out of the bed and began getting dressed. "I got some good stuff today. You're going to be happy. The camera loves you. Why aren't you acting at the moment?" "I have a full-time job as an assistant, and it pays great money, so it takes up a lot of my time." "Youth doesn't last forever, sexy man. Don't lose sight of your dreams." "I know, thanks. I won't." I grabbed all my stuff and he walked me to the door. "I'll send you the photos, we should do this again sometime." "Sure, that sounds good." I left his building and headed back to Hollywood.

CHAPTER 11

IMPERIAL: YEAR TWO

It took me a year of hard work to be initiated into the "family" and it had been almost as long since I had last pursued my acting. I would get auditions and would often be close to getting a gig but then became all too familiar with the art of rejection. Now I felt my life had become a movie. I found myself in a world where people pretended to like one another in the pursuit of their own personal agendas. The sequel to *Homicide III* was already in the works. The franchise was a cash cow, and it was important to milk it as much as possible. The sequel would follow the same format as *Homicide III* except have new characters and take place in a new city. After the Christmas holiday, Mike was still gone for an extra week. He opted to stay in Turks and Caicos, where he had been staying for the past two-weeks with his inner circle of friends and employees. Although in paradise, Mike was inspired with ideas for the new game and the holiday morphed into a work trip for everyone there. Brainstorming sessions were hours long, all the while Mike's nearest and dearest were missing out on the great weather the island had to offer. The longer he stayed, the better it was for me because the transition back into the office after a nice break was definitely much easier when he wasn't there.

Upon his return to the office in January, he walked in with a shaved head and an excellent tan. He looked like one of the criminals in Imperial's games. "J, in my office, now. Where's my water?" I grabbed the water off my desk, which I had waiting for him, as he entered. I closed the door and took a seat. "I am planning on buying a new place and I wanted to give you a heads up because you will need to handle all aspects of the move. I have been looking at properties and am scheduled to see quite a few this week." "I can get a head start on the research. Are there specific movers you have used or prefer?" "I don't deal with any of that. You figure it out. What you will definitely be required to do is pack all of my things and then have the movers pick them up, take them to the new residence and then you will have to unpack and organize everything." "How will I know what you will want and don't want?" "Don't get rid of anything unless I tell you to. If you are unsure about something, photograph it with your phone and show me. Otherwise, everything will go to the new place." I was working for the ultimate pack rat and I had to relocate his rat's nest to a new one. I think he wanted to move because he needed something new to be excited about. He had been living in the same house for several years and wanted more property and privacy. He wanted to plunk down onto his own estate, and he wanted to pay cash for the property. He had his sights set on Beverly Hills, Bel Air, and the Hollywood Hills. I didn't know all of this had been going on. Apparently, he had been viewing properties on his own. Somehow it seemed he was able to arrange those meetings without my assistance.

After viewing fifteen properties, he decided to drag me along with him so I could become acquainted with his realtor. I didn't mind because I was looking forward to seeing the posh homes. The search only lasted a few weeks. He opted for a massive, gated Beverly Hills estate that was modestly equipped with six bedrooms, 5 bathrooms, a sauna, screening room, indoor and outdoor gunite swimming pool, game room, movie theater, tennis court, koi pond and a meticulously landscaped garden. The $22 million dollar price tag wasn't daunting for him because he was "the man." Mike wasn't flashy and didn't flaunt his wealth, however, he did flaunt his demands and first on the agenda was for me to get a slew of boxes over to his current house and begin packing his life away.

Rather than having ninety days to close, he specifically requested to be in the new property in thirty days and had it written up in the contract. I had thirty days to handle this task and I needed every single day. For the next month, I had to spend five days a week and twelve-hour days in his house packing everything. I would put things away in boxes and label them with a list of what each box contained. The next day, I would return to find that many of the boxes were opened with things he needed that were then scattered on the counter, leaving me to repack them again. During this time, while I was at his place, Mike would call me to go and pick up lunch and dinner for him. I would have to take breaks in the midst of trying to move him. I was in Hancock Park and he would request food from a place in Hollywood, then ask me to bring it downtown to the office because I was faster than delivery services. I would place the order, and have it delivered to his house and I would drive downtown because I didn't have much time to spare. This would happen every day. I finally arrived at the third week of this fiasco and I could see the finish line in the distance. Mike basically wanted all of his things moved and I would have to put them away once everything was at the new place. He wanted to be able to walk into the new place and have everything organized so he could just go to sleep, and it would be as though he was already living in the new home.

Things surprisingly were running smoothly but I was exhausted. I didn't realize how much I hated moving until I had to organize someone else's mess. Moving day was finally here. It was a Friday and I had to be at his house at 8:00 a.m. I walked into the house and Regan and the three cats were running all over the place, clearly not sure what to make of all of the boxes. It was very quiet, I thought Mike had possibly gone to the gym since he often scheduled sessions directly with the trainer without my knowledge. I glanced in the bedroom from the living room and noticed he wasn't in his bed, but it was unmade. He had opened one of the boxes in the bedroom and I wanted to make sure that I packed it up by the time the movers arrived. As I walked into the room, Mike walked out of the bathroom completely naked. "Oh shit, sorry about that Mike," I said. "Fuck!" he shouted. He quickly grabbed a towel and rushed back into the bathroom. I couldn't help but laugh to myself when he ran in because I had just witnessed the smallest penis I had ever seen. And I had seen many. When he emerged from the bathroom, he was very uncomfortable. "Mike, I didn't know you were still here. I thought you already left." "Yeah, no problem." He was incredibly uncomfortable and quiet. It all became clear to me. The overbearing personality, the monstrous reputation, the infamous bark was all to make up for the fact that he had a small bite. "Do you have your set of keys to the new house?" "Yeah, dude, I have them." "I just wanted to make sure." "You know I have dinner plans and drinks after the office today so I will be home around 11:00 p.m. Make sure everything is perfect when I arrive." "I will," I said. By the way, Mike, since Ana is on vacation in Argentina, I thought it would be a good idea to have Lupita come and clean your new place. The house will be immaculate when you arrive." "Dude, whatever." He left for the office to raise another day of hell for the employees.

Today, it was my job to make sure the movers did theirs. I decided it would be smart to ask Lupita to help me at the new place. Not only could she clean but she could help me organize everything. Mike didn't care that she wouldn't be at the office because she was doing something to make his life better. Not to mention, it would save him money. Mike had asked me to let Ana go when she returned from her vacation because she was going to charge him too much for cleaning his new home. He felt that Ana should have been happy because she had a job. I was able to convince him that Lupita could clean his place on Fridays and spend half the time in the office and the other half in his home. That way, he wouldn't incur any cleaning expenses. Although he was wealthy, he also had his frugal side. He loved the idea and quickly embraced it as policy. I fired Ana when she returned. The movers arrived twenty minutes after Mike left. They marched in, were surprised at how organized all of the boxes were and began taking them out quickly. Two and a half hours later, they took the last box and were ready to take the entire truck to the new house. Shortly after the movers arrived, I sent Lupita to the new house with two of the cats and I followed in my car with Regan and Jason in his carrier next to me. When I arrived at the house, I opened the door, and I could see the two opened cat carriers on the floor. I knew they had already found their hiding places. I could smell the Clorox in the air and instantly knew Lupita was already at work in one of the bathrooms. The movers were two minutes behind me which meant I had to move quickly to figure out where all the furniture was going to go. Regan was already searching for the cats and decided that she was going to take a shit on the newly finished Brazilian hardwood floors. I immediately cleaned it up and decided to throw her in a large utility closet for the time being with her toys and food. The doorbell rang. The movers had arrived. Although I had kept all of the boxes in order, this task was a bit daunting and yet

I knew everything had to be perfect by 11:00 p.m. Mike kept the majority of the things he had so it was a matter of finding a place for everything and organizing it. Since this mansion was much larger, he would also need to purchase more furniture at some point to fill the rest of the house. As I was dealing with this drama, the office on the other hand, had its own action to contend with. A Christian group which was damning Imperial for exposing the youth to violent video games. Employees were informed not to wear any company T-shirts or hats, and they were instructed to enter the building through the back and have their ID on them at all times. *Homicide III* was up for several awards from a variety of outlets in the industry. This prompted the Christian organization to congregate in front of Imperial's office building. It was ironic that Imperial was getting gaming awards for their work while simultaneously dealing with protestors. Mike didn't give a shit about the actual awards. Other people would probably proudly display their awards in some way to illustrate their sense of achievement. Mike's awards all ended up in his storage facility. He believed that receiving awards made you lazy. If you got too comfortable being praised with statues that sat on a mantle, you won't continue producing epic games. During this move, I learned how bad Mike's hoarding was. Besides all of the promotional items, from the games and awards that were already at the storage facility, he kept many of the same items at his house as well. This included our video games from every country, T-shirts, magazines that Imperial and its games appeared in. The list was endless. I didn't even want to think about the storage unit right now and just wanted to get this move over with. I wore many hats during this move. Interior decorator was one of them. I had all of the movers place the furniture where I thought the pieces should go. I simultaneously arranged for the pool guy to come to clean the pool. The home was an urban oasis. Mike never had to leave his home and if he wanted to, he could work from home since one of the rooms adjacent to the screening room was about to become his home office.

Several hours later, the movers were gone, and Lupita had finished all her cleaning and helped me arrange some of the furniture. Some of the rooms looked as though they were staged for an *Architectural Digest* photoshoot. I still had an hour to spare so I sent Lupita home and continued to hang around. I decided to stroll around the house taking in what an amazing place it was. It seemed unreal, until my tour was interrupted by Regan's barking. I forgot I had put her in a utility closet. I opened the door and found her covered in her own shit and several puddles of urine everywhere except on the wee wee pad. She ran out of the closet and I chased her down so I could clean her up before Mike arrived. Once I finished with her, I placed her on the floor. I continued roaming around, feeling proud of the work I had accomplished. There was a haunting aspect of the house because it was also very empty. I looked at the time and still had thirty minutes left. I decided to take a dip in the outdoor swimming pool, and it felt incredible. I swam several laps and took a quick shower. I searched for the cats on every floor and made sure they were all accounted for. I fantasized that this was my home. I went downstairs when I heard Mike open the door. "Is everything finished?" he asked. "Yes, it is." I wasn't waiting for a thank you because I knew it would never come. "Why is that photo against that wall? I wanted it over there." He pointed to the opposite wall. "Fuck it all! I hate this place," he yelled as he grabbed a vase and threw it at the wall and then grabbed a second one shattering his $20,000 chandelier. I watched him self-destruct over all the drama surrounding the game. I figured the office must have been a nightmare.

"Is something wrong?" I asked, feigning ignorance. "Never hire your fucking friends to work for you! They are unappreciative pieces of shit." Besides the Christian group protesting, it turned out his outburst had to do with Tower Studios restructuring their deals. Mike and Rachael made sure they received much better deals than August, Gavin, and Liam, who was the Chief Technology Officer. They were livid that they weren't getting the kind of money that they felt they deserved. Mike had a private conversation with Jake Taylor to make sure that he and Rachael were taken care of. This incident began to cause a rift among his "family." His childhood friends began to resent him.

Although Mike created the ideas which built the brand that makes Imperial the cutting-edge leader in video game publishing, Tower Studios was the parent company that controlled the puppet strings. However, they always listened to Mike and ensured he was happy. "J, get out of here. Go home. I need to be alone." He didn't have to tell me twice. "No problem, Mike." I tried to get out of there quickly before he changed his mind. I didn't even care that he didn't mention that the place looked great, but I knew it did. "Hold on, before you go." I cringed and turned around and made every effort to display a smile on my face. "Get me a burger from In-N-Out and that will be all." The closest In-N-Out was in Westwood so I have to drive there and return. I walked to his refrigerator to make sure that there was Diet Coke and there was. I could hear Mike jump in the pool, and he began doing laps. I was drained and wanted to get home as soon as possible. I returned to Mike's about an hour and fifteen minutes later. He was seated outside by the pool smoking weed. "Mike, here is your food. I will head home now if that's all." "Thanks, dude, yeah, that's all. I will contact you if anything comes up." I left his place and finally ended my day. I arrived home, opened a bottle of wine, and I didn't even bother pouring in a glass. I started drinking it right from the bottle.

CHAPTER 12

E3

The entire weekend was a blur for me, or I was drunk the entire time. Monday morning rolled around and as I entered the office, I felt as though it had been a long time since I was there. It felt good to be back at my desk and in the mix of the other employees. They were all working on the next install-ment of the *Homicide* franchise and that's all that engrossed Mike's mind. The Marketing team had already created teas-er trailers and posters for E3, the annual main event in the video game industry. If you wanted to make a statement, E3 was the place to do it. The event was open to the press and the public, and all of the video game publishers converged to unveil upcoming video games competing for the spotlight.

The big push at E3 was going to be Imperial's game *Bad Boys*, based on the 1983 film starring Sean Penn about juve-nile delinquents. Imperial had acquired the rights to create the game from Universal Pictures and they had spent a lot of money to promote the launch which would take place at E3. They created a replica of a reform school and the dingy cells would be where the press would get to preview the game. I was able to see 3D renderings of what it would all look like at

E3. The industry and reporters were buzzing about the game and *Homicide IV*. The only thing that I knew so far, which had yet to be announced to the public, was that the location for the next game would be Chicago. Mike chose Chicago because of the high crime rate and all of the press surrounding the many shootings there. He wanted to capitalize and glorify it.

Mike walked into the office with August Brown. They were arguing before both went in the opposite direction to their offices. "This bottle of water isn't cold, get me another one," he demanded. I handed him his water and he asked me to join him in his office. I brought in my laptop thinking that this was going to be another lengthy request, but it turned out I didn't need it. "J, as you know E3 is a week away and I will need you to join me there. There will be a lot to get done." "Sounds good, I am looking forward to it." I was looking forward to being at the Los Angeles Convention Center for a few days. I actually enjoyed being out of the office so the change of scenery was going to be refreshing. Also, I'd get to see how the fans react to the excitement of everything going on surrounding the games. Although Mike stressed that it would be work. I had heard of past infamous events and dinners that took place during E3. Employees had to make themselves available twenty-four-seven for E3 to ensure that everything went off without a hitch. This included project managers, the entire marketing and PR departments and all the executives. There was a yearly tradition that everyone would have breakfast at Chateau Marmont before heading to the event.

When I arrived, everyone looked as though they were having a good time, but Mike arrived a few minutes after I did, and the mood changed rapidly. They didn't want to display an ounce of happiness because they knew Mike would think they weren't in work mode. I went inside to speak to someone from the Chateau regarding the private party we were throwing in a few days in the penthouse. We rented it a few days in advance as well in order to have the space to prepare. I was escorted by one of Chateau's employees who handled private parties. "How was your breakfast?" "I haven't eaten yet. The water was great though." We both laughed. "It's been a busy morning, but I will eat when I go back downstairs. I've eaten here before and the food is great." "Nice, well, we are certainly pleased that you like it." Her phone began to ring as we entered the penthouse. "Joaquin, I have to run downstairs but please just close the door when you are done looking at the space. Everything you had sent to the hotel should all be inside. Come see me downstairs if you have any questions for me." "Will do, thank you." I was in awe of the place. Everything I'd sent over was here. Mike had requested very specific items for the party and all of the boxes were counted for. I was distracted by the peacefulness of the white walls and the sunshine entering through the windows. The history of the love affairs, romantic evenings, and drunken stupors of Hollywood present and past could be felt. I sensed the old ghosts of Hollywood speaking to me through the walls. They were probably saying, "Quit working for this lunatic and get back to your acting." It felt nice to be around such history and at the same time the penthouse no less. I took a quiet walk onto the terrace and stood there briefly dreaming in solitude.

My phone began to buzz. It was a text message from Mike. *What's taking you so long? Hurry up! Everyone is halfway done with breakfast.* Once I returned downstairs, many of the employees had already left for the Los Angeles Convention Center. "Where were you?" Mike asked. "I was making sure everything you requested for the party was in the penthouse." I was starving. Everyone had already eaten, and Mike and Rachael were ready to leave for the convention center as well. I could see the remnants of the sausage and eggs that he devoured in the time I went upstairs. I wanted to grab a quick bite because I hadn't eaten. "Are we leaving now?" "Yes, we are leaving now. Why, did you want to lay by the pool and get some sun?" he sarcastically replied, with Rachael smirking in the background. "No, of course not, clearly I don't have a problem getting a tan. I am ready to work. You might want to put some sunblock on, you are getting red. Would you like me to buy you some?" "Let's go. Now." I couldn't help but laugh on the inside even though I maintained a serious face. I was starving so I wasn't exactly in the best mood. However, we lived in L.A. and eating was definitely not a priority. Marek pulled up as we were walking out. Mike wanted everyone to head out before him because he wanted to arrive a little later than everyone else so he could make an entrance. All of the geeks saw him as a god, and he was recognized by all of them.

When we walked into the crowded convention center, he immediately began receiving requests for autographs while Rachael was ignored. He obliged with a few but quickly walked to Imperial's space. The place was packed with just about every video game company who had new games to promote this year. Mike always ensured that Imperial acquired the largest space in the entire place and always generated the most buzz because of it. Imperial set the standard of how marketing should be done. This wasn't Mike's doing; this was all because of August Brown. To his direct reports he was a dick, but he was respected because of his ability to push his ideas to the limit and the company's marketing budget would set spending records. Within their space, Imperial created a juvenile detention center that contained six cells. The attendees could only see the entrance because the cells were only accessible to the V.I.P.s and the press who gained access to enter. Mike and August were pissed at one another. They maintained their distance and ignored each other while the game was being demonstrated on a large LED screen. The next day, Imperial would unveil the teaser trailer for *Homicide IV: The Windy City*, and the announcement for two other games. Everything was going extremely well. Mike was in a great mood. "J, is the reservation for my dinner with the fellas and the people from Sony in place?" "Yes, you're confirmed for dinner at Mr. Chow at 7:00 p.m." "Perfect, take the rest of the afternoon and evening for yourself. If I need you for anything, I will call you." "Really?" I said. I was in shock and almost didn't know what to do. "Make sure you're ready in the morning. Tomorrow is a big day." "Will do."

I headed home to take a shower so I could meet one of my friends for drinks. When I jumped out of the shower, my friend Oliver told me that he had to cancel so I decided to head out anyway. I was going to go to West Hollywood, but I remembered something a Lyft driver told me. He was a screenwriter and he said he would go to the bar at the Beverly Hills Hotel for networking purposes and he would go every other day. I decided I wanted to do the same thing to see if I could meet anyone influential in the film business. I walked into the bar and noticed a few stools open. As I sat down, another man was about to sit down on the other stool. "Oh, I'm sorry, is someone sitting here?" he asked. He was tan, muscular, very attractive, around six feet tall with dark straight hair and green eyes. "No, it's free," I said. He smiled and I immediately recognized him, although he had no clue who I was. "What are you drinking?" "Belvedere and soda." He turned around to the bartender and ordered my drink and a whiskey for himself. "Where are you from?" I asked, even though I knew exactly where he was from. "New York. And you?" "I live in Hollywood," I said. "What is your name?" "My name is Evan. And yours?" "My name is Seth." I gave him an alias and he did so in return. I was beginning to enjoy our game. We were in L.A., the land of make believe so what better time than to perfect my acting skill?

He was Jake Taylor, the CEO and founder of Imperial Game's parent company, Tower Studios. I remembered hearing he named the company Tower because he saw himself as superior looking down at the competitors. Right now, I didn't care about any of that. I just couldn't believe this was happening, but I gave him no indication that I knew who he was. No one else at the bar would, he was just another attractive face. The only reason I knew what he looked like was because I saw a photo of him with Mike when they vacationed together on a group trip to Antigua. There were also photos in Mike's house when I helped him move. He, however, had no interaction with me so far because he was rarely in the L.A. office despite having an office on the floor above Imperial's. He often worked from his mansion in the Hamptons and took a helicopter into Manhattan because he had an office and apartment there as well. I had heard that he was an avid collector of classic and rare cars and maintained a house in Los Angeles which housed many of them. "I'm curious, what is your ethnic background? You don't look Mexican, and you could be Middle Eastern." "I'm Puerto Rican." "Not many of you here in L.A. besides JLo and Benicio del Toro," he said and laughed. I couldn't help but laugh as well. "Why are you out alone?" he asked. "Technically, I am no longer alone." "What are you looking for?" "Why are you here alone and what are your plans this evening?" I asked. Knowing very well that he had a wife and two kids back East. "I was in the mood to grab a drink. My flight was delayed, and I missed a business dinner at Mr. Chow. I am looking for a good time and I love coming to this hotel's bar," we both laughed. "Can we go to your place?" he asked. "No, my roommate has a date over." I handed him another lie. "Where are you staying?" "I have a house here." Jake, or I mean "Seth" seemed in deep thought for a moment "Would you like to come over?" he asked. "Sure, why not."

We walked into the bar separately, but we didn't walk out alone. The valet pulled up with his car. A beautiful black BMW. He drove up to the Hollywood Hills to an incredible ultramodern home that was a work of art. At this point, I was more in awe of the home than of him. We walked into the entryway, which had a modern cement bridge with koi fish on each side up to the door of the home. Although the home was not mine, it felt like it was. Home sweet home. It was the residence of my dreams and hopefully someday would become my reality. "Make yourself comfortable."

The house was decorated with a fusion of ultra-minimal and modern furniture. "So, why don't you come here more often? Your house is amazing." "My wife hates LA. I only use this house when I'm in town or when my wife throws a fundraising party on the West Coast for one of the charities we support." "Would you like some wine?" "Sure." While he poured us both glasses and opened a glass sliding door that led to the pool, which was lit and heated. I took my clothes off and jumped right in. Seth emerged from the house with the two glasses of wine. "I see you got a head start." I swam over to him at the end of the sixty-foot infinity pool. The lap felt like an eternity and at the same time I felt like Michael Phelps. I drank some wine, leaned up out of the pool, and gave him a kiss. He then took his clothes off and jumped in.

CHAPTER 13

WAKING UP IN
THE HOLLYWOOD HILLS

The next morning, I woke up in an extremely comfortable bed with crisp white Frette sheets. Jake was lying next to me naked. I stared at the ceiling and realized I had slept with the boss, not my direct boss but more importantly, Mike's boss. I quickly and quietly moved off the bed and began the scavenger hunt for my clothes. I found them downstairs on the cement near the pool. I was so tempted to go for a morning swim, but I didn't even know the time. I put my jeans on and realized my work phone was missing. I checked my jacket, and my personal phone was inside the pocket. "Oh shit." I looked for my work phone and couldn't find it. I was sure I had several messages from Mike waiting for me. I looked all over and still couldn't find it until I noticed something at the bottom of the pool and sure enough it was my phone. I jumped in and grabbed it, hoping it wasn't destroyed and that it was actually water resistant. I had no clue if Mike had tried to contact me.

At that moment, I was grateful for having to carry two phones. I dried off and got dressed. I walked through the living room quietly as I didn't want to make any noise so we could avoid the awkward morning after. I sat on the sofa putting my sneakers on and noticed remnants of last night adorned the floor. Empty wine bottles, three to be exact. Three condoms on the floor along with a bottle of lube. I plugged my phone with a charger Jake had in the kitchen and nothing. The phone was dead. Luckily, I also carried my personal phone and I ordered my Lyft. One would arrive in fifteen minutes. I decided to wait outside so I could make a quick move into the vehicle when it arrived. Somehow I thought if I stood outside, the car would come faster. I was wrong. Luckily Jake was still in a deep sleep. Finally, ten minutes later, the car arrived. I managed to figure out where to buzz the gate open and I walked out. "What took you so long?" I asked, annoyed. "Are you kidding me? This house is practically hidden in the hills, and the signal is shit." I ignored him. "I need to get home as quickly as possible." "Ok, you got it." As he pulled up to my building, I quickly exited the car. "Hey, thanks, have a great day." the driver said as I closed the door and ran into my building. It was now thirty minutes before I had to be at the convention center, so I needed to hurry up. From my personal mobile phone, I checked the voicemail of my work phone and I had six messages. I'm sure they were all from Mike. "Where the hell are you?" he yelled on the first message. "Joaquin, call me back as soon as possible," message number two and this continued until the sixth message where he just hung up. I called him right away. "Hi, Mike, it's Joaquin." "Where the hell were you? I was trying to reach you last night?" "Were there any emergencies? I made sure to take care of everything before I left." "Yes, I couldn't fucking fall asleep and I had a craving for In-N-Out again." "Ok," I remained silent. "My phone died, something is wrong with it." "Well, you won't need it. Marek and

I are downstairs. Come down now." I was frozen. I couldn't believe he was downstairs but I looked out my window and sure enough there was the Escalade. "I'll be right down." I didn't have a chance to shower so I took a whore's bath and sprayed some cologne on and got dressed. I rushed downstairs and entered the vehicle. "About fucking time. What happened to your phone?" "I dropped it." "Well, get a fucking new one, stat, unfucking believable. Anyway, in two weeks we have the first ever Imperial Esports event taking place in New York at Madison Square Garden. I wasn't going to have you come but I changed my mind. I'm also speaking on a panel of video game publishers and the film industry at the Tribeca Film Festival." "Sounds good." I didn't get too excited because I knew this was going to be a work trip. "Why are we headed to Beverly Hills?" I asked. Marek looked at me in the rearview mirror. Mike was consumed with his phone and punching away at it furiously. I figured we were heading to the convention center where everyone else was that morning. Finally, I received a delayed response. "We are going to The Ivy for breakfast." I didn't have a problem with that because I hadn't eaten. "Did you make that reservation? Because you didn't ask me to make it." "No, I didn't. We are meeting Jake Taylor there. His assistant, who is reliable, took care of it. It was a last-minute meeting; Jake is heading to New York later today."

My heart started to race because I couldn't believe this was happening. I had an amazing evening with Seth, who I knew was Jake, but now I was finally going to be properly introduced to him as Joaquin, Mike's assistant. This was going to be awkward, to say the least. We arrived at The Ivy and Mike immediately jumped out of the vehicle and I reluctantly followed. "Hello, gentleman, welcome to The Ivy." We were greeted by a very blonde, tan and polite hostess. "J." Mike said. That was my cue to speak with the hostess. Mike didn't like dealing with the little people. "Hi, I'm sorry, the table should be under Jake Taylor." I said. "Ahh yes, Mr. Taylor is already here, let me show you to the table." "Thank you." Mike proceeded as if with blinders on, completely oblivious of his surroundings. He just wanted to be taken to the table and start the breakfast meeting. He walked in front of me so when we arrived at the table, Jake had yet to see me. "Enjoy your lunch gentleman," the hostess said. "Jake, you fucker. How are you man? You flaked out last night, what happened?" "I had something unexpected come up." Mike and Jake shook hands and did the very heterosexual half-embrace. When they did, Jake looked at me and he looked as though he had seen a ghost.

"Mike, who is this?" he asked in shock and disbelief. "This is my assistant Joaquin. Joaquin, this is Jake Taylor, the founder of Tower Studios. The man who believed in my vision." "Yeah, except when you've had too much scotch," Jake said, trying to add some humor to the situation but clearly still in shock. "Jake, what the hell is wrong with you, you look stone faced," Mike said. "No, no, not at all. I just can't help that Joaquin looks so familiar to me." "I get that a lot," I said with a smile. "He's Latino, it's L.A. they're fucking everywhere," Mike chimed in. Jake's face turned from inquisitive to extremely concerned. "Ok, Jake, you can't have my assistant. He works for me, plus he is useless sometimes. Your assistant is a piece of work, I hope for fuck's sake you're at least fucking her." "No, I'm actually faithful to my wife." I smirked and looked at the menu.

Mike began talking business and I was supposed to sit there and listen. He didn't mind that I listened to their conversation. I already knew a lot of information, and he trusted me and was past the point of paranoia with me. He underestimated me. I sat there, listened and learned. They spoke about the fact that an outside investor was interested in purchasing Tower Studios. Mike didn't want any part of this because he wouldn't have the control that Jake allows him to have now.

I learned quickly that it was a give and take relationship between the two. Imperial was a cash cow for Jake, so he definitely wanted to keep Mike happy and give him the creative freedom to do whatever he wanted because at the end of the day, he benefited from it. If someone else took over the company, they wouldn't be as generous to Mike as Jake was.

I zoned out of the conversation for a moment and scanned the restaurant. I noticed Gwyneth Paltrow at one table with an unidentifiable fit man. Most likely her trainer making sure she doesn't eat any carbs. At another table, Simon Cowell in an obscenely tight T-shirt displaying his moobs while eating with a woman who couldn't keep her eyes off of his chest. Our waitress returned to take our order. "Can I get you gentlemen some beverages?" "Coffee, black please," Mike said. "I'll have a Mimosa," Jake said. "Make that two," I said. Mike turned to me. "You are not going to be drinking on the job, are you fucking kidding me?" he said. He turned to the waitress. "He'll have a coffee, black, as well." "Mike, you're kidding, bring him a Mimosa too," Jake stepped in and told the waitress. "Thank you," I said as Mike gave me a dirty look. Mike excused himself to go to the restroom. "What do you want?" Jake said in a serious tone. "What do you mean?" "Did you follow me last night? What are you up to?" Jake was suddenly paranoid about what my intentions were. The world must have felt too small like it was closing in on him. I grabbed the sparking water and poured some into my empty glass. "I didn't follow you last night. It was more of being at the right place at the right time." "Cut the bullshit. You knew who I was the whole time. How much money is this going to cost me?" he said without showing too much emotion due to his Botox. "Well, this isn't something we have to resolve now. We can revisit this conversation. I'm going to be around for a while." "Don't hold your breath, especially working for Mike. Don't tell anyone about last night if you want anything from me." "Understood," I said as Mike returned and sat back down.

They continued to talk about business. The waitress appeared and asked us if we were ready to order. I ordered lobster on a bed of mixed greens and a hint of lemon. Mike ordered a carnivorous lover's lunch of a burger and fries while Jake went for the same salad I had. We were all starving. Mike devoured his burger in three bites, and he looked like a horse with a mouth full of hay except his mouth was filled with French fries. He continued to speak to Jake with his mouth full and I completely zoned out what he was saying because I couldn't stomach what a pig he was. Jake may have been grossed out by Mike's table etiquette or lack thereof because he ate his salad quickly. Or he had other things on his mind. "Alright, we have to get going. I want to see how things are going at E3. We can continue this when I'm in New York," Mike said. "I have a couple of meetings, but I will be jetting back to New York, so I won't be going to the convention center. You have everything under control with E3. I will take care of this," Jake said, referring to the check. "Ok, thanks man," Mike said without the slightest hesitation or movement to grab his wallet. "It was nice to finally meet you, Joaquin. I'm sure I'll see you around," Jake said as he shook my hand with a very firm handshake. "It was nice meeting you as well," I smiled and walked off with Mike. Marek pulled up and we were off to the convention center.

CHAPTER 14

E3 DAY TWO

We arrived at the Los Angeles Convention Center and Imperial's correctional facility replica for *Bad Boys* was a visual spectacle in itself. It was much more crowded than the previous day. The fans were lined up to have mug shots taken of themselves. They wanted to feel a part of the Imperial world. As I gazed over the line, the sea of men and women in Nintendo and Zelda T-shirts wouldn't be convincing as criminals but video game fans they were. Mike and I entered the structure and the wardens stepped aside as I entered with the god of the gaming punks. We walked into a section where August was hosting more V.I.P.s. It was supposedly a who's who of the video game industry, but I didn't know any of them. However, some of them were big wigs in the industry. They were geeky, many overweight, prematurely aged guys. Mike was pleased with their reactions, which were overwhelmingly mouths open in amazement with slight drool exiting the corner in excitement. They demonstrated additional missions in the game and also screened the trailer for *Homicide IV: The Windy City.*

After a short time, Mike, August, and I walked over to another section that was designed to look like an interrogation room. This would be where the press would be allowed to personally interview Mike. Charles Santos, August, Raul Perez, the president of Imperial Latin America, and myself remained in the room as well. I had to stay in case Mike needed anything. Charles Santos stayed to keep the interviewers moving along, while August added some bits of information whenever Mike would let him get in a word. Raul also gave his thoughts and talked about Bad Boys as well and how it was a game that would resonate with the Latin American market. Although Mike wanted to maintain street cred and have an aloof reaction to the press, he relished the moments where Imperial's games were admired and being gushed over. Which translated to a shit load of money come release time. At the office he was inaccessible, but at E3 he was a cheap whore getting his fix. One by one, journalists were allowed in and they each treated Mike like a celebrity who understood them. He knew exactly the type of games they wanted to play, and he made sure they were created. Mike knew how to turn on the charm when he needed to. One of the reporters asked him about his reputation for having a volatile temper and his less than stellar treatment of his employees. Mike brushed it off as rumors. One reporter said that murder, mayhem and crime have been taken to the next level and Mike's eyes lit up as in approval signaling him to please write just that. I kept thinking that the minute we walked out of the convention center, the monster would resurrect again to destroy another day.

Five hours later, I had zoned out after hearing so many of the same questions and had my eyes fixated on the trailer for the game. It was dinnertime and I was starving. The last reporter wrapped up interviewing him and there was one more hour left of the event. "J, let's go," he said. I kept thinking how much easier life would be if he had a wife or a girlfriend. Instead, he opted for paid encounters that fulfilled him sexually but made him a needier person for me to deal with. "Where to now?" I asked. "I'm going to have Marek take me home and I need you to make a reservation at Craig's for the entire team for dinner and then to the Chateau to celebrate a successful E3." I didn't hear anything he said after he wanted me to make a reservation for the entire team at Craig's for twenty people in less than two hours. Craig's was a classic West Hollywood hot spot, so this task was going to be impossible.

He boarded the SUV and sped off as I waited for my Lyft. I called the restaurant and they thought I was joking. They weren't going to be able to accommodate a large group like ours on such a short notice. Especially since Mike wasn't an A-list Hollywood star. I started searching for restaurants and availability. Finally, Paley in Hollywood was able to fit our group in. As soon as I did, Mike called. "Did you confirm the restaurant?" "Yes, but we weren't able to get into Craig's on such a short notice. I made a reservation at Paley instead." "It's not what I asked for but fuck it, you've disappointed me before, let's not end your streak. I'll meet you at the restaurant and don't be late." I arrived at Paley thinking I would be slightly early. Everyone, with the exception of Mike, was already there and seated. They left the head of the table empty for Mike and of course the seat next to it was empty for me because no one wanted to sit next to him. I sat directly across from Rachael. "Hi everyone." "Hi Joaquin, what happened to getting Craig's?" "They couldn't get us in." "That's too bad, we are seated with everyone instead of having a private room" she said.

Mike walked into the restaurant and made his entrance dressed in shorts, a polo and sneakers. He plunks down into his seat. "Fuck, I'm starving." "I was just telling Joaquin what a shame we couldn't get into Craig's," Rachael said. "Don't get me started on that, I'm too fucking hungry," Mike said.

I sat there in silence and passed him the bread. "Rachael, I think you should visit mom and dad in Florida after our trip to New York. I'd go but I need to be back here," Mike said. Rachael was visibly annoyed. "Why the hell do I have to go? I have a lot to get done as well." Mike pointed to her and forcefully showed her who was in charge as if Rachael didn't already know. "You are going. I need you to do this and that's it." Rachael remained silent and resembled a small girl being scolded by her father. Mike being the big brother, and not to mention the man who signed her paychecks and handed her a career clearly controlled her and she hated it.

The drinks kept coming and everyone's mood was more relaxed as the night progressed. Mike grabbed Raul and hugged him and told him that he could never leave the company, he was family. Everyone smiled and laughed and seemed to go along with it, but I found it weird, insecure, and completely needy coming from a man who walked around as if he didn't need anyone. Raul looked rather uncomfortable with the exchange, being a machismo Latino, but he went along with it and told Mike exactly what he wanted to hear. That was a pattern I recognized over time. Mike was happy as long as you told him what he wanted to hear. If you told him otherwise, he would smile at your face and hate you behind your back. He sloshed drinks and became increasingly obnoxious. "You guys are all my fucking family," he shouted. The last time I checked, I was Puerto Rican and none of these people were my family members. I enjoyed the evening while silently analyzing everyone's behavior.

I remained under the radar by not saying too much and definitely not drinking too much. I hoped that Mike wouldn't come near me to ask me if I was going to work for him forever because I would have to bite my tongue until it bled out to avoid saying, "Hell no." It reminded me that my dream was in fact to become an actor. Not to be at Mike's beck and call for the rest of my life. Food was ordered to subside everyone's buzz, but the drinks outnumbered any amount of food that adorned the plates. When we wrapped up the dinner, I decided to walk ahead and step out to get some fresh air. I could feel the California breeze massaging my skin.

Everyone emerged and we all headed to the Chateau, where we would continue to celebrate in the penthouse suite. We walked in and a full staff was waiting for us, including servers, and I went to the balcony drinking while hypnotized by the city lights. Suddenly, I heard a lot of commotion coming from inside. They were cheering on one of the employees. When I looked again, I realized there was a mountain of Cocaine on the table and Mike was pushing Brad's face into the pile. "Snort it like a fucking man, not like a pussy!" he shouted. "Treat it with respect. That's fucking Everest, now climb you fucking asshole." Brad felt obligated to snort and snort he did. Maybe his balding head would grow back some hair. The party went on for hours until everyone passed out. Mike had Marek pick him up and take him home while everyone else was draped around the suite. It was a scene out of *Animal House*. It was a hell of a mess that the cleaning crew was going to have to clean up. It was 4 am and I was about to head out when Brad emerged from the bedroom. He was drunk and coked up. "Joaquin, where are you going? Let's party dude." I didn't say a word as I just wanted to go home, but he persisted. "Come on, dude, let's go." He was so smashed he had no clue what was happening. I requested a Lyft, and our driver was two minutes away, so I decided to head downstairs with Brad. I managed to get Brad semi-coherent enough to walk down the stairs and into our Lyft.

We were headed to the last gay sex club left in Los Angeles. Brad began to doze off in the car. "Brad wake up, we are going into the club." We handed over our IDs at the entrance. "Hi, two please. I paid at the front desk and they handed me condoms and lube. Brad was stumbling but I helped him up and we walked upstairs. There was an entrance to a corridor that was a maze of open and closed doors where I could hear men grunting, getting off and lingering, waiting to invite someone in. There was an empty one. I walked in with Brad and set him down on a platform. I stripped him of his shirt, exposing his worked-out torso and helped him take off his pants. He was so out of it and he passed out. I grabbed the condoms, placed them on his chest along with lube. "Have fun." As I walked out, there were guys in the hall watching me as I entered and left the room. "Are you looking for fun?" a chubby, hairy man asked me. "No, but my friend is. He's a bottom but make sure to go easy on him. He's fresh out of the closet." His eyes lit up in excitement, as if I just handed him a cheeseburger. I walked away as four other men went inside with the man. I decided to walk home which was only a few blocks away.

The next morning, I was at the office preparing for Mike's arrival. Brad rushed to my desk immediately. "Good morning, Brad, did you have a great time last night?" "Fuck you. You fucking asshole, you left me in that place. I'm not gay." His voice kept raising and then whispering to contain the anger he was experiencing. "Well, I'm sure that's changed now that you've popped your cherry," I said. "I finally came to when a guy was fucking me up my ass without a condom. I pushed him off and he zipped up his pants and said he was the eighth guy who had a piece of me." "Why did you do that to me?" "I learned you fucked up my chances of getting into the PR department, so I fucked you back. Literally. Well, not me. A fat, hairy guy and several others." "Don't fucking tell anyone about this." His eyes watered up in anger and shame. "Your secret is safe with me. It looks like you learned your lesson. Don't fuck with me."

CHAPTER 15

NEW YORK FUCKIN' CITY

Several of us were getting ready to head to New York and I was excited because I was going to extend my stay and spend some time on Fire Island for the weekend at a friend's house. That was until Mike said that he needed me to be on-call during the weekend in L.A., so I would have to return with him. The employees that were headed to New York included everyone who was in attendance at E3. They were scheduled to fly out on American Airlines. I was aware of this because I had to book everyone's flights through Judith. However, Mike, Rachael, and I would be flying in a private jet into Teterboro, New Jersey. He preferred taking jets, especially when others were footing the bill. I was going to take a Lyft to LAX, but Mike wanted me to stop at his place at 6:00 a.m. I drove into the driveway and parked my car. I sent Marek a text to get his ETA when my phone began to ring. It was Mike. "Where are you?" "I'm downstairs." "Come inside, now."

I walked into his home and saw leftover take-out on the large kitchen table, mail piled up, and clothes thrown on the sofa. The remnants from his weekend. "Come upstairs." I ran up the stairs and Mike was pacing back and forth in and out of his walk-in-closet, grabbing clothes and stuffing his Tumi luggage. He continued to grab things from his drawer and started throwing them at me. "Here, put this in the duffel." I continued to help him pack as we were thirty minutes behind schedule now. "Did you arrange for Lupita to take care of the cats and Regan?" "Yes, she will be stopping by." "That's fine, the cameras are all activated, yes?" "Yes, they have been since you moved in." "Good, so I can watch her to make sure she isn't robbing me." "She will arrive this afternoon and will stay the weekend to make sure the house is cleaned as well." The chandelier Mike destroyed was also going to be replaced while we were gone. "Marek is outside." "Good, take the bags down and let's go." I was looking forward to this trip because it was my first time flying in a jet. I sat in a seat towards the front while Rachael and Mike sat further behind me. They barely spoke a word to one another on the flight. I fell asleep. All of a sudden, I felt someone tapping my arm. "Wake up, this isn't a fucking vacation." Mike was waking me up making sure I was ready to go. "J, grab my bag and bring it out," Mike said. "Oh, mine too, Joaquin, thanks." They were already in the SUV when the driver helped me with their bags.

We were headed straight to Manhattan and to The Standard Hotel in the Meatpacking District. We checked in and were told that everyone else was having breakfast at The Standard Grill. I wanted to go straight upstairs and relax for a little while before we headed to the Tribeca Film panel, where Mike would be speaking. "J, have them take our bags up to our rooms and let's go see everyone, I want to make sure they aren't treating this like a fucking getaway." I asked the front desk to send the bags up and the three of us went to the restaurant.

We saw everyone laughing and enjoying themselves and as soon as they spotted Mike and realized we were approaching, each of their smiles disappeared like dominoes and they were all silent. "I'm glad to see everyone arrived ok. I want to make sure you all realize we are all here to work and I expect 150% at the events. Don't stay too much longer." All three of us walked out. "I'm going to my room. Let's meet in a few hours before this talk." "Sounds good," I said. "Perfect, I'll see you both later," Rachael said. I went upstairs to my room and just stood against the glass staring at the city. It was a beautiful spring day. I received a text on my phone.

Hi Joaquin, it's Jake. I know you're in town with Mike. I want to speak to you at some point. Hi Jake, Sounds good. Let's plan something when you are free and when no one is around.

I decided to lay down on the bed and I began to fall asleep.

****

I started running because I was being chased except, I couldn't see the person behind me. I just saw darkness. I continued to run and run until they caught up to me. The mysterious figure began punching my face, but I still couldn't see who the person was. The person grabbed me and threw me through a glass window, and I began to free fall. As I fell and landed on my back. I jumped up and propelled myself up from the sofa. I woke up from the dream.

****

I felt groggy and startled. I looked at the time and I had only been asleep for thirty minutes. My phone rang. "Downstairs in fifteen minutes," Mike said. I jumped in the shower and quickly got dressed. As scheduled, the six SUVs were downstairs. We all boarded and headed to the BMCC Tribeca Performing Arts Center. Mike had a button-down shirt, jeans, sneakers and a baseball cap that said Imperial in all caps. We finally arrived despite hitting some traffic on the West Side Highway. Mike had to do the red carpet. Everyone went inside to take their seats but Rachael and myself waited as Mike spoke to various reporters. There weren't many since this was a video game panel and everyone who was taking pictures were definitely gaming fans, tourists, or people thinking they were going to spot real celebrities. He plowed through the interviews and we headed inside. Our team was assigned to the first two rows, and Mike went to the back to meet with the host and the rest of the panel. They waited about twenty more minutes to ensure that the venue was filled to capacity. The lights were dimmed, and the talk was about to begin.

"Hello and welcome to Tribeca Talks. I'm your host Chris Hardwick and we have several people on deck here to discuss the gaming world and how the industry has grown to become even larger than films. Games have evolved from the 8-bit classics we knew as children to the cinematic story-filled plots that make them masterpieces today. We welcome several of the kings of the gaming industry who've released epic games that keep us gamers playing for hours." I was already zoning out of this talk. As each panelist spoke, from Mike's demeanor you could tell he thought they were all beneath him. He gave them his semi-automatic grin. The smile that he put on when he hated people, but he tried to conceal it but only anyone that knew Mike would be able to notice. Everyone on the panel was talking about the gaming industry and plugging their games and now it was Mike's turn for more questions.

The panel was quite boring up until the point they started taking questions from the audience. "Mr. Chapman, I'd like to know how you deal with the controversy surrounding the *Homicide* franchise and the press it received for the hidden sex scenes?" Mike, visibly annoyed but trying to contain himself, responded, "We fucking press on, we move forward and focus on the next game." And another question for Mike. "Mr. Chapman, I'm a mother of two sons and I'm here not as a fan but I'd like to know, do you have children? Your games are offensive and should only be available to adults." Mike was boiling. "As I've said before, we are in the business of entertaining people and my games aren't created for your children. I have a question, where do your kids get the fucking money to purchase the games? I'm not in the business of raising children, I am in the business of making money and no I don't have any fucking children." "How about a question for one of our other panelists?" Chris said. Another audience member stood up. "Mike, I just want to say that I think your games are awesome. I heard a rumor that your company is a front for a drug business and that's why your games are so authentic, because it's the world you live in every day. Any truth to that?" "Fuck off with your rumors. That's fucking ridiculous." Mike stormed off the stage. I along with the other employees walked out after him. We went outside and he had already jumped into the waiting SUV and left. We all assumed he retreated to the hotel, so we decided to return as well. I went to the front desk and they confirmed they saw Mike go upstairs. I figured I would let him have his tantrum without me around for a change. He wasn't texting me which meant he didn't want to be bothered.

I went to my room and started to get myself ready to go out. I was in the mood for some trouble. I headed to Boxers in Hell's Kitchen. I walked in and headed straight for the bar and ordered my drink. "Hi, can I get Belvedere with club soda and a lime." The shirtless bartender nodded and handed me my cocktail a few moments later. "Hi, what's your name?" I turned around and it's a tall, attractive guy, with dark hair, brown eyes and a perfectly trimmed beard. "Hi, my name is Joaquin, what's yours?" "My name is Vlado." "What's your background?" "I'm Serbian." "Nice, I like your name." "Thanks, it means 'born to rule'." "And do you?" "Oh yeah and I'd like to rule your fuckin' body." I broke out laughing but at the same time turned on because I couldn't keep my eyes off of his sculpted body, which was obvious with the perfect fitted T-shirt he had on. "Well, technically you can't rule my body, you can conquer it, if you have the stamina." "I would conquer it and if you were mine, I

would rule." Anyone else would be turned off by his posses-
sive mentality but it just kept making him hotter. "Where do
you live?" he asked. "I live in Los Angeles, you?" He took a sip
from his beer bottle. "I live around the corner; do you want
to come to my apartment?" "Yes."

We arrived at his one-bedroom apartment on West 51st
street. He lived on the third floor of a six-floor walk-up. Immediately after entering, he offered me a drink. "More vodka?" "Sure, that sounds good." He grabbed a beer from the
fridge and began preparing my drink. "You don't have anything on your walls, paintings or pictures." "Yeah, I prefer to
be a minimalist. There's enough to see in this city. When I
come home, I don't want to be surrounded by more images.
I want to chill." "I get that." "Let's go to the bedroom." He
grabbed a remote and put some music on which happened to
be a song by Imagine Dragons. "Is this okay for you?" "Yeah,
that works, I love Imagine Dragons." Vlado placed his drink
on the nightstand and immediately began taking his clothes
off. "Get comfortable." By comfortable he meant completely
naked. He didn't have to tell me twice. I set my drink down
and then my clothes were on the floor. We began having
hot sex. It was passionate and we kissed each other as if we
both meant it. We went several rounds and kept taking short
breaks to hydrate with our drinks. We were in every position
and going from rough to gentle and back to rough. By the
end, we were both exhausted. We fell asleep, I was the little
spoon, and he was the big spoon.

I woke up the next day and all of sudden my phone was
vibrating like crazy. I noticed I had several missed calls from
Mike and text messages as well. *Where the fuck are you? We
are leaving the hotel for The Garden in ten minutes. Your ass
better be there.* "Fuck!" I jumped out of bed. I sent Mike a text
just to let him know I was on my way. *I'm stuck in traffic. I
woke up early to run some errands before the event. I will be
there.* "Is everything ok?" Vlado asked. "I have to get to work.

Can I take a quick shower?" "Of course." I took a shower and as I was quickly lathering up, he stepped into the shower with me. He began kissing the back of my neck and we went one final round before I needed to leave. Once we were done, I finished rinsing off and I stepped out. I quickly dried myself and got dressed while he remained in the shower. I walked back into the bathroom. "It was great meeting you." I kissed him. "Same here, hopefully we'll run into each other again." "Take care."

I walked out and my Lyft was waiting for me downstairs. I began looking at the news on my phone. I checked to see if there was any press from the previous day at the Tribeca Film Festival, and there was. "Mike Chapman Has Epic Meltdown in Tribeca," "An Imperial Fall, Imperial President Can't Take The Heat," and the headlines continued. The driver made it to Madison Square Garden in less than ten minutes. I pulled up to the theater and walked in. I immediately saw Rachael on her phone, and she spotted me. She stopped her conversation. "Where the fuck have you been?" "Traffic was a nightmare." "Everyone is inside." As I walked away, I could hear Rachael tell whoever she was talking to "just take care of it." It was probably her assistant, so I brushed it off. I walked into the theater and it was set up for the gaming competition. It was interesting watching all of these players compete while playing *Homicide III*. It was like a battle royale of players trying to take down the other one in the world created by Mike himself. Mike immediately saw me when I walked in. "You've mastered the art of fucking up." "I'm sorry, traffic was crazy." "You can't fucking disappear and not be available when I contact you. The point of having an assistant around is to assist and to do what I ask. These aren't leisure trips; I'm running a fucking business." "I assumed you didn't want to be bothered when you left the event yesterday." "I didn't, but you still have to be available, you are the hired help and it's never a good time to be a fucking slacker." I remained quiet instead of going on the path of a never-ending conversation where getting through to him would be impossible. I stood and watched the competition as the fans were enjoying themselves as if they were watching a basketball or football game. Visually, it was amazing to see all of the games on very large screens and gamers trying to kill each other off.

A few hours later, the winner had been crowned and Mike had the duty of going on stage and handing him the trophy and shaking the winner's hand. Once that was done, we could leave. I wanted to get back to Los Angeles as soon as possible. I was hoping that the success of this event would diffuse what occurred the night before. However, the Esports event didn't garner as much press as the outburst at the film festival did. There was nothing much to celebrate at this event and everyone felt as though they were in limbo because Mike wasn't happy. I received a text from Jake.

I'm not going to be able to meet up with you while you're in New York. We'll have to do it another time. Hi Jake, Not a problem. We'll talk soon.

Everyone retreated back to their hotel rooms and the ritual of having dinner to cap off a successful event wasn't happening this evening. The next day we would all return to La La Land.

CHAPTER 16

STEPHANIE

I sluggishly walked into the office on Monday morning and wondered why the sun didn't follow us back. I can't stand June gloom in L.A., but it was fitting for the way things were at the office. I began going through my emails and came across an email Mike forwarded to me. He would forward emails to me because he wasn't sure what the sender wanted, or he didn't want to be bothered. In this case, the email he received was from a woman named Stephanie. She worked at *Stiletto Magazine* which was in Miami. It was a long email, which is why Mike didn't read it, but she was asking him out on a date. I wondered how a woman who worked at *Stiletto Magazine* had enough time to pull herself away from a shoe obsession to sniff Mike out in the video game industry. Especially one on the opposite coast.

I decided to do some research on her before Mike arrived. According to Google, her mother made a name for herself thirty years ago in Germany for being a party girl and an infamous gold-digger. She was able to sink her claws into two multi-millionaire husbands, leaving her the ability to live the life of leisure dividing her time between Miami, Argentina, and Spain. The apple definitely didn't fall far from the tree. Stephanie was a twenty-eight-year-old features editor for *Stiletto Magazine*, which meant her biological clock was ticking, not to mention she was trying to set herself up for life. She probably wanted to prove to her mother that she paid very good attention to her mother's lessons of life and love.

She was approaching thirty, which to heterosexual women, meant she needed to hook on to some poor schmuck soon before her looks and body were shot to hell. Then again, the pictures online showed an average looking woman, nothing special, colorless skin that has prematurely aged, and she wasn't that petite. I had to hand it to her though, she was definitely on the prowl for the right man. Mike was so needy that he would most likely fall for this ploy and think with his dick instead about his bank account. I quickly skimmed the rest of her note where she ended with the suggestive line. "I'm in L.A. on assignment this week. Let's have dinner and maybe dessert while I'm in town." She wasn't exactly playing hard to get. In every photograph I saw of her online, she was wearing designer outfits. They must have been given to her courtesy of her mother, men or maxed out credit cards. I printed the email and placed it on Mike's desk so it would greet him when he walked in. He was uncharacteristically late this morning, and I didn't have any emails from him. However, I was sure he would pop in any minute. His phone began to ring. "Imperial Games," I said. "Oh, I'm sorry, I must have the wrong extension," she said. "Who are you looking for?" I asked. "Mike Chapman," she said hesitantly. "This is the right number, but he is not in the office yet. May I take a message?" "No, it's alright, I will speak to him later. Thank you," she said and quickly hung up. My first introduction to Stephanie and I could smell the desperation. She didn't even give Mike a chance to contact her, and she was hungry for his multi-million-dollar dick.

I heard Mike coming in through the corridor. Today, he actually had a genuine smile on his face, and I cherished it. "Good morning J," he said, energized as he strutted into his office. He didn't demand his water as usual. He didn't know it yet, but I was sure he would be getting laid again soon. That is if he was receptive to Stephanie's proposal. He was rich and happy on the outside all while being vulnerable, lonely, and horny on the inside. "What the fuck is this?" he asked as he grabbed the printed email off his desk. "It was an email that came through. I figured you should take a look at it." I said as I handed him his chilled water. "That's not cold enough, grab me another one." I walked out of his office as he kept reading Stephanie's note. I watched his expression, which, as I predicted, was a good one. I walked in with a bottle of water that was the same temperature to the touch as the last one I returned to my desk and he quickly closed his office door and grabbed his phone. I tried to read his lips without being too obvious, but I could see that he was visibly coy and nervous. Ten minutes passed and he emerged from his office even happier. I couldn't think of any other time I saw him this excited, but I knew it was only a matter of time before it disappeared. I think he smelled the pussy in the air. I just smelled tuna. "J, make a reservation for two at Nobu Malibu for Thursday evening at 8:00 p.m." "Will do." He turned around to address me. "I will have further instructions for a couple of things I will need you to do before then." "Ok," I said as I nodded. I could only imagine what these demands would entail. Last time I arranged an evening for him, he was fucking a prostitute. Now a gold-digger had her sights set on him. He should just keep seeing Shana. It would be cheaper and a lot less drama. I observed him talking to Rachael possibly about Stephanie because he was showing her the printed email. I glanced over towards Gavin's desk and realized he was also watching what was going on as well.

Two weeks earlier, Gavin skipped out on E3 because Mike wanted him to remain in San Francisco to ensure that developing projects were moving at a much more rapid pace than they were. Mike viewed the guys at Imperial San Francisco as lazy bums. Although Gavin wasn't in L.A. for E3, he wasn't very far out of sight since Mike called and emailed him constantly. Word around the office was that Gavin was exhausted from being Mike's bitch. Gavin had been in San Francisco for long periods of time overseeing Imperial's zombie franchise Jugular. He wasn't able to sustain any type of social life or normalcy in Los Angeles due to his constant traveling and long stints away. All of Gavin's relationships were one-night stands. Gavin knew that what Mike needed was a woman in his life and that he couldn't fulfill all the duties that one would. Well, at least all except have sex with him. Mike would call Gavin at all hours of the night to discuss business, but it was more of a mask for the fact that Mike was incredibly lonely. He couldn't stand to be alone which was part of the reason he hired some of his childhood friends to be part of his company. He needed that sense of security and at the same time that power. He had a penchant for hiring as many friends as possible into his company; it didn't guarantee that they were going to be treated well. Financially, yes, but otherwise they were moving targets in Mike's mind. He could at any moment explode on any of them. This was his defense mechanism. He allowed very few people into his world but as the saying goes, "You always hurt the ones closest to you." Gavin Kent was definitely no exception. Mike even thrived on humiliating him.

A month ago, Gavin had not been feeling well and Mike kept insisting that Gavin tell him what was wrong. He confided in Mike by telling him that he had an STD, and Mike decided to share it rather loudly in a comical fashion with the entire office. Gavin was humiliated, but at the same time his hands were effectively tied. He knew he had to stay at the office as long as possible because he had just purchased a house in the Hollywood Hills and needed to hang on until he felt it was time for him to leave. His weathered face every morning said it all. Dark circles under his eyes and red eyes he needed to soothe with eye drops. He went from having a great complexion to exhausted. The perils of being Mike's bitch. Mike loved it and because he was single, he didn't have any alternative than to bully Gavin, and Gavin was a glutton to the punishment. He took it and it even seemed as though it was affecting his dog. His dog suffered from separation anxiety because Gavin was hardly ever around, and he had to board her often because Mike would purposely send him on business trips to oversee things in the San Francisco office and attend meetings in Latin America. Mike did this to get back at Gavin for getting the dog because the dog was taking attention away from him and Mike didn't want anyone competing with him, not even pets. Gavin pleaded with Mike to allow him to bring his dog into the office since Mike always had Regan around. Gavin used the excuse that Regan and Max could play together. That was how the "bring your dog to the office policy" started. Soon, the office was inundated with dogs because others began to request to bring their dogs to the office since they were hardly ever home either. Mike obliged but warned everyone that if there were any accidents or issues, their dog would have to remain at home. Gavin was fed up with Mike because he didn't have a life of his own and his attempts at a relationship with his many girlfriends wasn't going to happen with Mike constantly being so needy. My assisting him subsided a bit but not by much. Gavin was on a mission to get Mike a girlfriend.

Mike wasn't exactly the approachable type, and you couldn't tell he had money by looking at him. He was the guy that many women passed right by on the street or only had a one-night stand with, not because he was ugly but because he dressed like a bum and wasn't very hygienic. On a bad day, he looked like a serial killer, and on a good day a serial killer. Gavin started spreading the word to many of the females of his past to see if they knew of anyone that he could set Mike up with. Apparently, no one in L.A. was biting so Gavin reached out to the many well-heeled women on the East Coast and the South. Gavin was a manwhore and yet never pretended to be otherwise, which is why he remained popular and in demand. If a woman needed to get laid, Gavin was their man. The buzz had been going around the network of models, stylists, editors, communications executives and television hosts.

Gavin finally received a call from one of his "regulars." She was the Editor-In-Chief at *Stiletto Magazine*. She was the female version of Gavin, so had no interest in settling down and no need. She owned a penthouse condo in South Beach and a villa on the island of Turks and Caicos. She did have a features editor who worked for her that she couldn't stand and thought what better way than to get rid of the entitled bitch than if set her up with a rich man on the opposite coast. "Hi Gavin, it's Iona from *Stiletto*." "Hi Iona, how've you been? "Very busy, but I've got a girl for Mike." "Really, who?" "She is a features editor who I am trying to get rid of. She is a spoiled pudge of a thing." "Is this someone you actually like? Or not?" He asked. "Does it matter? Do you like Mike?" "Fair enough." "Okay, how are we going to set this up? Straightforward is best. He has a low attention span," Gavin said. "I have an idea. What's Mike's email? I will tell her to send him a note. I'm going to send her to Los Angeles on an extended assignment so it will be the perfect opportunity for them to meet and get to know each other." "Alright, sounds good, make it happen." "Oh, I will. I always get what I want," she said. "Well, since Mike is going to be taken care of, how about we get together again?" "Gavin, I've had you and frankly, you aren't man enough for me. I'm into real men. I lost interest in you the minute I saw Mike yell at you a year ago at Balthazar, in New York, as if you were his child. I like men, not timid boys. I have to go." She hung up.

Although Gavin felt rejected, he also felt good because he had a victory. He possibly found a match for Mike and he was hopeful that it would be the case. Mike didn't have any prospects and his ex-girlfriend was a painter who wasn't shy to get into fist fights with Mike. They were a match made in heaven because she matched Mike punch for punch. When the relationship grew old and wasn't working any longer, they both found it difficult to end it, so Mike did the only thing he knew. He bought his freedom by writing her a check for $500,000. They both knew what it really was, but they lacked communication skills when it came to getting in tune with their feelings. She took the check and ran. In Mike's mind, it was money well spent. Since then, he had been alone and relied on hookers, mainly Shana. With all of his success, however, he felt the pressures of settling down and being with just one woman. He didn't have a lot of patience at all or charm to win over a woman and he was always so work obsessed. He only had the cash, but in Los Angeles, that's all it takes. Mike had a packed schedule for the week, but he was behaving as though he was getting ready to attend the Academy Awards. He had me go to the store and get him razors, clippers, toenail clippers, a new toothbrush, mouthwash, baby wipes, condoms. He was going all out for Stephanie. He was being more hygienic than usual. I bought him all the items while he worked out at the gym. He wanted to be pumped up for his date. I left all the items for him on his kitchen table. He was definitely going to have to spend some money on Stephanie to get her to accept his small package. I had a feeling she wouldn't mind. I left his home, hoping that his date on Thursday would go well and that it would develop into something more because maybe, just maybe, he could change.

CHAPTER 17

AND THEN THERE WAS... LOVE?

The next few weeks consisted of Mike wooing Stephanie. He wanted to impress her, shower her with gifts, and get laid in the process. Not necessarily in that order. Her boss had apparently extended her assignment in Los Angeles, so Mike sent me out on shopping trips to purchase a Chanel handbag, shoes from Christian Louboutin, and a few dresses from Chloé. On one particular day, I was giving his bedroom a makeover because he sent me to the Frette store, on Rodeo, with the direct order that he needed new bedding because Stephanie doesn't like to sleep on beds not draped in Frette. The shopping sprees and honeymoon phase went on for almost six months.

Although he was extremely wealthy, Mike was both frugal and simple. Eventually he would either grow tired of Stephanie's pussy, or he was going to take the relationship a step further and she would realize that all the attention and spoils she was receiving were merely a mirage for the real Mike she would eventually encounter. Mike finally decided to unveil

Stephanie to his "friends" at Imperial. He asked me to make reservations for twelve at a Korean BBQ restaurant in Koreatown. This time, I had enough notice to request the private room, but it didn't matter, we were slumming it because Mike wanted a casual, fun night out. This was going to be everyone's opportunity to meet Stephanie. So far, everyone was looking forward to meeting the woman that was putting Mike in a slightly better mood than usual. I was able to make a reservation at the very last minute because one of the owners was a friend of a friend.

When I made the reservation, Mike told me not to make any plans on Thursday night because he wanted me to come out as well. I didn't mind because I knew there was going to be drama simply because there always was. I wanted to see how Stephanie interacted with everyone else. This wasn't going to feel like work so much. It was going to be an opportunity to watch how they all get along and if his closest confidants put on a show of how much they liked or disliked Stephanie. I already didn't like her. The others, including Rachael, haven't had the chance. Mike always felt he had the right to be involved in everyone's personal life and strongly vocalized his opinions about their relationships and whether or not he approved of their choices in spouses or significant others. However, when it came to himself, he was very private until he was sure that he wanted to introduce Stephanie to everyone. I arrived at the restaurant twenty minutes early to ensure that everything was in order at the restaurant for the booking and Mike's arrival. After confirming that all was set, with the hostess and the room, I walked directly to the bar. A drink was absolutely necessary.

I sat at the bar and asked the bartender for a Belvedere and soda. This was going to be a long night, so I knew I needed to prepare for it. A few sips of my drink and Gavin walked in, probably with the same idea I had. "Hi Gavin," I said as I looked at him and then returned my stare to the bar. "Hey man, how are you?" He greeted me and looked at the bartender. "Can I get a Scotch on the rocks, please?" The bartender quickly placed the drink in front of Gavin and we both drank leisurely and continued to stare forward and at the same time increased our drinking pace as the time drew closer to everyone's arrival. "I'm fine, thanks. You must be a lot better now that Mike has Stephanie." "Yeah man, I'm so happy they are working out." "Do you expect drama tonight?" "Always," he said as he slurped down the last sip. It was as if though he gave his directorial cue for everyone to enter as he made that statement. Everyone arrived with the exception of Mike and Stephanie. Mike needed to make an entrance even though he pretended not to be obnoxious.

We all headed to the private room and decided to take our seats. Everyone instantaneously requested cocktails while I ordered my second drink. A short time later, Mike walked in with Stephanie. He was dressed in a navy sport coat, khaki pants, boots and a chocolate newsboy hat while Stephanie decided to get glammed up. It appeared as though she was going to walk the red carpet in her unflattering, tight fitting Herve Leger dress. She shouldn't have felt any pressure because if Mike liked her, then everyone else did. Only Rachael would have the guts to tell Mike that she didn't like her. Hopefully she would tell Stephanie that wearing the dress was her first mistake. Stephanie said hello to everyone as if she was the First Lady and bullshitted us by saying she had heard so much about us. I was the last one she greeted. "Oh sweetie, thank you so much for putting this together. Mike raves about you." "Thanks, it's a pleasure to meet you." I kept thinking that now that he had met her, maybe she would start walking Regan and I wouldn't have to take care of the bitch.

As the drinks came in, Stephanie turned to the waitress and requested a Prosecco and Mike asked for a draught beer. Everyone was talking shop and discussing video games, and Stephanie looked bored out of her mind. I was too, because

I was ready to witness some action. When everyone finally looked at the menu, we ordered a little bit of everything. The beauty of Korean BBQ is that you can either have someone cook it for you, especially when you are in a large group, or you can turn it into an interactive experience, and everyone can cook what they are eating. I sat back embracing the intoxicating feeling as the vodka kicked in. "J, I think you should do the honors." "What honors?" "You should do the cooking." "I'm a terrible cook." "You'll do just fine," he said.

I began turning the meat as everyone else at the table continued their conversation. Stephanie looked at me. "Sweetie, can you make sure not to overcook the beef?" Did I mention I hated her? Not because she didn't eat well done beef but because she had the nerve to instruct me on what to do. She wasn't a picky eater since she carried a bit of excess weight that not even her dress could contain. "Sure sweetie," I replied. "You're taking too long." Mike said after two minutes passed and I was still cooking everything. "I like to make sure that it's all cooked through." "Here give me that," he said. "I'll show you how it's done, watch and learn." Mike cooked everything a few minutes more and the beef had a pink color to it. "Okay, it's ready," he said. He placed the meat on a plate so everyone could pass it around and everyone put some on their plate, with the exception of me, Christina, and Annabel. We requested salads. Stephanie jumped in at the chance to devour the food her man prepared for her as if it was a primal representation of her love for him. Being a non-red meat eater, I passed. I ate as much kimchi as possible as I waited for my salad. "You are my fucking family." Mike said in a gluttonous manner. "Acceptance into this family is a life sentence." Here we go again, I thought. Every time he gets drunk, he speaks about the honor of being part of the Chapman family and how it was a life sentence. Honestly, I wanted my death sentence now.

Between the raw meat being devoured and the insecurity in the air, I was nauseous. The men all ate like Vikings and so did Stephanie. Turning to Christina, Anabel and me, she said, "I admire you three so much for not being meat eaters. I couldn't do it." She stood up immediately after and started to toast the group. "I love all of you and am so happy I could be a part of the Imperial Family." She toasted with Mike's beer in hand and ordered another round of drinks for everyone, of course because she wasn't paying. I don't think Christina and Annabel ate much of anything in general, except perhaps their inner thoughts. An hour had passed and by the time dessert arrived, everyone was drunk. I spaced my drinks out with water, so I wasn't feeling much of anything except restlessness and a strong desire to leave. "J, you can leave. You have done a great job tonight. Go home." Without hesitation, I stood up as many looked envious as I was just provided a pardon. "Thanks, Mike. Have a goodnight, everyone." I smiled and walked out and left Koreatown. I rushed home and went to bed. I couldn't help but to think that it appeared that Stephanie won everyone over. However, that was after several cocktails. The next day I arrived at the office and most of the group from the night before, including Mike, had to call in sick because they had food poisoning. All except me, Christina and Annabel. The day was a quiet one. I sat at my desk and the phone rang.

"Sweetie, I need you to go to the store for me and pick up some Imodium or Pepto-Bismol." "Who is this?" I didn't recognize the voice. I couldn't tell if it was a man or a woman. "It's Stephanie. Mike and I have diarrhea from the food last night. Food poisoning. We are so exhausted and can't leave the house. Can you go to the store and get us that, along with a copy of *US Weekly*, *In Touch*, *Entertainment Weekly* and *Vogue* and when you get here take Regan back to the office with you. She is out of control." "Ok, no problem." I left the office and ran the errands for Stephanie and Mike. I wasn't crazy that the request came from her and not Mike. It was only a matter of time before she thinks I work for her, which I don't.

When I arrived at Mike's house, I couldn't help but smell the overwhelming stench of lavender and marijuana. Then I realized the weed wasn't only to soothe Mike's appetite for cannabis, but also to mask the undeniable odor of shit because the lavender wasn't working. The cats were nowhere in sight, but Regan ran to me as if pleading for me to save her from the air that was tightening her throat. I could hear flushing coming from both bathrooms and Mike screaming in pain from the other bathroom. "Hello, I'm here." "Bring me the medicine," Mike shouted. I placed the magazines on the kitchen table. I slowly walked upstairs to the master bathroom door and he opened it quickly, grabbed the bag and closed the door. "Thank you, now go back to the office." I gladly turned around and exhaled. I headed towards the kitchen and Stephanie was there waiting for me. I didn't think it was possible, but she looked even paler than the day before. "Sweetie, here is the list of some more things we need." I grabbed the list which spanned the entire page of the college ruled paper. I was not only doing grocery shopping but also some personal shopping for Stephanie, which meant I was stopping at Whole Foods, CVS, Sephora, as well as doing several tasks, including arranging her and Mike to get deliveries from Juice Press so they could cleanse. I also had to go to Chinatown for some herbs that I am sure she read about in *InStyle Magazine*.

What initially appeared to be a quiet day was now turning into a hectic one. Not to mention that I had to take care of Regan who preferred taking a shit indoors. The first thing I did when I left Mike's house was take her straight to City Dog Club so she could play with other dogs and I wouldn't have to worry about her. I then went into the office briefly and the second I stepped out a downpour ensued. This was probably the second time it's rained in L.A. in five years. I didn't have the luxury to take a pause in my day. I bought all of the herbs they requested and drove to Whole Foods next. Once I checked that off my list, I continued.

Four hours later, I was back at Mike's house to drop off all of their items. Or Stephanie's mainly. I went upstairs and Stephanie was sprawled on a sofa, in the media room, watching a marathon of reality television while Mike was nowhere in sight. She picked herself up off the couch and signaled for me to be quiet. "Mike is sleeping," she whispered. Sweetie, thank you so much. Will you be a lifesaver and put all those things away?" She threw herself back on the sofa and returned to her television program. I doubt Mike knew this side of her, since she was always playing the supportive girlfriend role doting on his every move. He was frequently high on weed so I'm sure he wouldn't even notice unless it directly affected him. I was sure it would eventually come to light. I put all of the items away and didn't say another word. As I closed the last cabinet door it was as though she knew I was finished. "Thanks, Jay Jay." "Excuse me?" "I said thank you, Jay Jay." "My name is Joaquin and that's what you can call me." "Oh, I'm sorry did I offend you?" "If you call me Jay Jay again, then yes, you will." "Oh, ok. I'm sorry sweetie." "I will bring Regan back at the end of the day and will you please stop calling me sweetie." "I'm so sorry, thank you so much." I didn't respond to her and I walked out of the home. She felt bad but at the same time seemed taken back by the fact that I wasn't a member of the staff that she was going to name to her liking.

The following day, Mike called me into his office. He was sitting at his desk with August Brown by his side. "Stephanie told me what happened yesterday, and she told me you told her not to call you Jay Jay." I thought he was upset with me, but at that point I didn't care. "Yes, I did. I don't wish to be called that or sweetie and I let her know." "Good man, job well done," he patted me on the back. "Thanks." I smiled and walked out of his office.

CHAPTER 18

MEET MOM & DAD

Six months had passed, and the company was doing extremely well. Mike was moving quickly with Stephanie. Within a short time, she had already given up her short-term apartment in West Hollywood, quit her job, and moved in with Mike. She was so happy because she didn't have to take care of herself anymore. She had a man that could do it for her. Not just any man. As of this week, he was number ten on *Forbes's* list of the "Ten Most Powerful People in Entertainment." She did well for herself, but she had yet to seal the deal. She wasn't pregnant or married.

Mike's parents were arriving in a few weeks. They were going to meet Stephanie for the first time. Mike wanted to introduce them to her a few months ago but it took that long to convince his mother to take time away from her estate and stable of horses. She loved riding and owned several horses. She was a former psychiatrist who married a doctor but loved her horses more than anyone. Stephanie was excited but also dreading meeting Mike's parents. She was working out with a trainer three days a week. She had a hair appointment, manicure, and pedicure scheduled. She also went shopping at Chanel and Marc Jacobs because she needed to look perfect for Mike's mother.

The day of his parent's arrival, Mike wanted me to go with them to the airport. I felt that this was a moment and experience for them to do on their own, but I was more than happy to come along because I wanted to see what the interaction was going to be like between Stephanie and Mike's mother. Mike's mother was good friends with an ex of Mike's, Emma Adams, who briefly worked at Imperial. Mrs. Chapman considered Emma the daughter-in-law that got away. The trip to the airport was nothing short of drama. Mike and Stephanie couldn't stop fighting because they were both stressed out. Mike wanted the meeting to run smoothly, and Stephanie felt the pressure Mike was putting on her. Mike definitely cared what his parents thought, although if they didn't like Stephanie, I was sure it wouldn't stop him from seeing her. He had been speaking about her for months, but when his parents found out who Stephanie's mother was, they were less than thrilled that Mike was dating Stephanie. They didn't know her mother personally, but they knew of her through their high society social circles. Mike's parents were from West Palm Beach and Stephanie's mother was from Miami, where she resided in a lavish mansion thanks to her first husband. Stephanie's mother's reputation preceded her.

We waited near the baggage claim area for his parents to arrive. I stood in a daze, half-awake with my Tom Ford sunglasses on, a gift from Mike, and I was still wondering why I had to be there. I knew I was a personal assistant, but this was too personal. Even with Stephanie in tow, his future ball and chain, he felt the need to have me there because I'm sure I would be tasked to do something for someone. He was definitely a private man but when I was around, he was not shy about displaying his true colors. "You could have put on a fucking dress." Mike snapped. "It's 7:00 a.m. and we are at the airport, we aren't going out to dinner for fuck's sake."

Stephanie wore tattered jeans which probably took her fifteen minutes to squeeze into, black Chanel flats, Marc Jacobs T-shirt and black Wayfarer sunglasses with her hair up in a ponytail. Garden party Valentino, it was not. "Whatever." I remained quiet, pretending not to hear them speak. "Joaquin, do you think I look bad?" They both stared at me waiting for me, to side with one of them. "You look comfortable." "That's not what I asked." "He thinks you look like shit, too. Drop it, it's too late now."

He walked away as people began arriving as their flight had apparently landed. "He is such a dick," Stephanie said as she turned to me. I continued to remain silent and felt like I had been here before. Then I remembered I felt as though I was conversing with Brenda. I seem to be around women who despise the men they are with but do nothing about it for some reason or another. Stephanie's reason was clearly monetary. Mike spotted his parents, and they were very pleased to see him. "Mom, Dad!" Mike approached his parents. His mother wrapped her arms around him as if he were a little boy again. For a second, she humanized him just by illustrating that there was someone that actually gave birth to and loved the monster. He shook his dad's hand and gave him a hug, showing more reserved and composed affection towards his father. They definitely appeared to be opposites. She was well preserved and seemed to have a sweet demeanor to her with a clear fashion sense. She had her hair in a bob and dressed in a Dior pantsuit and black patent leather Christian Louboutin shoes. She took one glance at Stephanie from head to toe, and her mouth opened in amazement. "Hi, darling," she said to Stephanie and kissed her on each cheek. "I saw photos of you, and I must admit, I thought you'd be thinner in person." I laughed and Stephanie hit me on the arm. Stephanie gave her a fake smile and then Mike's mother introduced herself to me. "You must be Joaquin. I have heard so much about you. You have great skin." She gave me a hug. "Are you making sure my Mike is staying out of trouble?" "Yes, ma'am." I smiled. This car ride back to the house was going to be interesting. His father introduced himself to Stephanie. "So, you're the young lady my son has fallen for," he said as they hugged each other. Stephanie's face looked at peace as Mike's father appeared to provide her with a warm reception. The sense of relief was visible on her face. "I thought you were going to be taller in person." Her smile disappeared quickly. Stephanie was crashing and burning with the folks so far. "Alright, let's go, let's go," Mike said, rushing his parents and trying to change the subject.

We walked to his new black Range Rover. Today, there would be no Marek. I was shocked when Mike asked me to meet him at his place because he was going to drive to the airport. He wanted to make sure that he was the one to pick up his parents so there weren't any fuckups. I sat in the back seat in between Stephanie and his mother. I was the Berlin Wall, circa 1990, it wasn't going to be pretty between the two. "I love your hair, Mrs. Chapman," Stephanie said, trying to win her heart. "Thank you, dear, my hairdresser Mikael is divine," she said behind her Louis Vuitton sunglasses. She lowered them for a moment to glance at Stephanie's hair. "You don't go to the hairdresser much, do you? I wish I could be that simple." "Mom! Be nice," Mike chimed in from the front. "It's alright, babe. I haven't had a chance to go in a while, I know it looks horrendous," Stephanie agreed with Mrs. Chapman as her self-esteem crumbled. "Tonight, for dinner, I will blow it out," she said. "Oh dear, a woman mustn't leave the house without being well presented. It shows a lack of self-worth." Stephanie laughed but her aggravation was clearly visible. If I wasn't sitting in between them, this would have turned into an Alexis and Krystle fight from an epic Dynasty episode. Can anyone say throwback? Stephanie wasn't a Krystle, though, so Mrs. Chapman would be Alexis and Stephanie would be the maid who does well for herself by sinking her claws into a rich oil tycoon. Unfortunately for Mike and Stephanie, traffic was at a standstill. Mike's father was quiet, yet he struck me as an excellent observer. "Mrs. Chapman, I understand you were a psychiatrist," I said. "Yes, I was a Psychiatrist for many years, but I'm retired from that and now I focus on riding my horses and philanthropy. I was always very independent. I think it's important for a woman to be her own woman, have her own career and not depend on a man. Don't you agree, Stephanie?" "Mom!" "I understand you quit your job, is that correct?" she asked. "Yes, that's correct, I'm now managing our home." "Oh dear, that's what the staff is for and I didn't raise my son to date the staff." Stephanie couldn't and didn't say a word. Her pale face turned red as she held back a mouthful. I smiled and looked out of the window as I watched the sunshine bright on a beautiful Los Angeles summer day. "What are your goals Joaquin?" "I am an aspiring actor." "Do you want to starve?" Mike interrupted. "Quiet, that's nonsense. If you are passionate about it, follow through with it," Mrs. Chapman said. "You're not leaving me so forget about it," Mike said. I gave him a fake laugh as if I felt appreciated, but I knew his sentiments were more out of selfishness.

He believed that anyone who worked for him shouldn't have any aspirations other than making his games better, his pockets deeper, and supporting him and the brand. Otherwise, they were not loyal family members. In Mike's world, there was no such thing as having dreams and passions that didn't involve his games or vision. Finally, the traffic was moving and all of us in the back seat were very quiet. Mike and his father were in the midst of a lengthy conversation about Florida, and his father was giving him updates on family friends in their neighborhood. We arrived in Beverly Hills with the exception of Stephanie's ego. It was left behind somewhere on the freeway.

Since everyone arrived safely, my only task at this point was to make sure that all the bags were brought in and taken to the room that his parents would occupy. I placed their bags in the large guest room. Mrs. Chapman quickly followed me because she wanted to see the room for herself. "Sweetheart, you can take Mr. Chapman's bags to another guest room. This one will be mine. We don't sleep together, I can't deal with his snoring and at my age, I need to get as much sleep as possible to keep the wrinkles away. That and a good dermatologist." She winked.

I couldn't get over how much more sophisticated Mike's parents were than he was. He obviously had the means for luxury but was always understated walking around in the same white T-shirts, jeans and sneakers. His parents were definitely not walking around in casual attire. I think it was Mike's way of rebelling. He also felt that he needed to maintain credibility because of the violent street games he was known for, he couldn't walk around in a top hat and suit. Mike wanted credit for all of it and wanted people to believe that he was a street savvy guy from Florida despite being raised in country clubs and private schools. His tough attitude was in contrast to his childhood being cared for by nannies and an overprotective mother who didn't allow him to get too dirty as a child. He was spoiled and honed his skills as a bully and practiced on his little sister who would become his shadow, following him all the way to Imperial Games. Once I left the bedroom where his mother would be staying, I made my way quickly downstairs so I could get on with my day and actually enjoy myself. "Joaquin, I'm in my office." Mike beckoned just as I was two feet away from my escape. "I'll be right there." I backtracked to see what he wanted. I walked right in and he was at his desk in front of his computer. "I need you to make some reservations. Dinner for four at Nobu in Malibu and lunch at Chateau Marmont." "Will do. I will email you with confirmation of those reservations."

"Okay, that's all for now. Make sure your phone is on in case of anything." "Sure thing."

I left his house and headed east towards my place which feels more like a hotel room these days since it feels like I don't spend that much time there anymore. I called Nobu and Chateau Marmont to confirm they had availability. Nobu was booked solid but I was able to get him a table at Chateau Marmont. I had another call coming in and it was Mike. "J, did you book my reservations?" "I'm in the process of doing that now. You're on the waitlist for Nobu, they are fully booked." "Do I have to do everything my fucking self?! Can't you do anything right? Why the hell am I paying you so much money if you can't get something as a simple reservation squared away for me? Fuck my life." He hung up the phone and my blood began to boil. I didn't hear from him for the rest of the day or weekend. I was sure on Monday he would have more anger to blast off at me since he spent the entire weekend with Stephanie and his parents.

I walked into the office and it was oddly quiet. I grabbed his bottled water and placed it on my desk. I stepped out briefly to get him his Nitro Cold Brew and when I returned, I placed it on the kitchen counter and noticed that no one was around. I opened the top, spit in it and mixed it in and placed the top back on it. Fifteen minutes and I heard his heavy footsteps stomping into the office. "In my office now." I walked in behind him and handed him his coffee and bottled water. "This is about the only thing you have gotten right in the past five days." He threw the bottle against the wall and it exploded open and all over the sofa. "Make sure that gets cleaned up." "Is that all?" "What do you mean is that all? Watch your fucking tone with me." He continued to slam things and I stood there stone cold. He wanted me to be fearful, but I stood there not flinching once. This infuriated and frustrated him further. "Just get out." I made it a point to show him that I was not intimidated and had him figured out. I analyzed and dissected him, in my mind, and I learned how to deal with him. He was no longer a puzzle I needed to decipher. He was an insecure and needy person who needed to be managed.

I walked out of his office and called Lupita and asked her to dry the water off the sofa for me. She was on her way into his office, and he stopped her and quickly made his way to my desk. "No, I don't want her to clean it, I want to see you do it." "I always thought the whole point of having a cleaning lady was to have her clean." "It is, but I want you to do it this time and don't question my authority. I'm the fucking boss here." He walked back into his office so he could have the last word. I told Lupita that it wasn't necessary for her to clean. She sensed my frustration. "¿Está bien?" she asked. "Si, gracias, todo esta bien." I went into the kitchen and reached for the paper towels. Then I noticed that Rachael had made one of her fruit smoothies and the blender was filled with the purple concoction. I grabbed the blender and walked into Mike's office and closed the door so no one would be able to hear us. His back was towards me. "Is this what you had in mind?" I took the blender and poured the smoothie all over his sofa. "What the fuck are you doing?" He lunged at me and took a swing at my face. I ducked and punched him in the stomach. We began to fist fight and yet no one outside had a clue because the shades were down. We were punching each other, until Mike couldn't take anymore. We both had bloody faces. "You fucking asshole. No one has ever stood up to me that way. Not even Rachael. Have Lupita clean the mess up." "Does that mean I'm fired? Or am I going to have to sue you?" I was prepared to lose my job at that moment, but I also knew I had him against the ropes. I stood up and began wiping the blood from my face. "You just earned yourself a $20,000 raise." "I believe the number you were thinking of was $40,000 and I'm taking the rest of the day off." "Fine, get out."

I emerged from the office with a bloody face. Employees were horrified. Many of them had open mouths and stone faces as Lupita panicked. "Mijo, qué te pasó?" Simultaneously, a tester walked towards me with concern. "J, dude, what happened?" he asked. "I'm fine. I just had my employee review." I went to the bathroom, cleaned up, placed my sunglasses on my face and went home.

CHAPTER 19

THE NEXT DAY

The next day, I arrived at the office later than normal. Mike was already there and didn't say a word to me. He had a few bandages over his left eye. I had scrapes and bruises that I was nursing as well. I gave him his bottled water. "Thanks, man." "You're welcome." While there was a lot of gossip in the office about what went down, Mike and I went on business as usual. Some people were saying that I should sue or quit. Mike was pissed off since his parents did not like Stephanie at all. He overlooked our fight because I had already crossed over the family threshold. I looked at the clock and his calendar and realized he was scheduled to meet with his trainer in twenty minutes. He rolled down the blinds to his office and changed into his gym attire. He definitely needed to work out some stress because he was unbearable. "I'm off to the gym." I sat at my desk and scanned across the office.

The faces of the underpaid, overworked and underappreciated were now those of the executives who basked in the extreme wealth they acquired thanks to Mike. The problem was that Mike always used this to make them feel as though he owned them. They didn't have lives of their own because their lives belonged to the company. This control was a prison where the prisoners sipped on Veuve Clicquot and indulged in caviar because they could. The day dragged on and he didn't return and didn't ask me for anything.

The next morning, I received a text instructing me to come straight to his house because we were going to take his parents back to the airport. I survived the week with his parents in town and absorbing his emotions but at the same time returning it right back to him. He told his mother that he had gotten his bruises after stopping a mugger who had just taken a woman's purse in DTLA. "Hi J." Stephanie said. "Hi Stephanie." "Oh my God, what happened to you?" Mike jumped in and spoke for me. "He was with me when we stopped the mugger." "You are both heroes. You must be careful Joaquin, you can't damage that pretty face of yours," Mrs. Chapman said. "I will Mrs. Chapman, thank you." Mike and I glanced at each other and went along with what she was saying. "Shouldn't we get going? I wouldn't want you to miss your flight," Stephanie said. "Joaquin, would you like some coffee?" Mrs. Chapman asked. "Stephanie, be a darling and fetch us some coffee while I change," she said. "Joaquin, I want to show you a photograph we are going to need to be displayed in the dining room," Stephanie said. We walked over to the formal dining area. She pulled my arm and quickly I knew this had nothing to do with the photograph. "His mother kept asking me if I was the type of woman that wanted children. She said usually party girls from the fashion industry don't exactly want to be mothers nor do they make the best mothers. I mean, we aren't even married yet and she is asking me how I feel about children. Then she had the nerve to say my body doesn't look like the type that would bounce back easily from pregnancy. Mike tells her to stop, in a casual manner, but he didn't protect me from her verbal assault." I stood there quiet as her eyes were tearing up and yet I had no sympathy for her. However, I had to play the game. "Everything will be fine; mothers are always tough on women because their sons are their babies. She was testing you to see how tough you are and if you could take what she dished out at you. I'm sure by the end of it, she liked you." "You think so?" I lied straight through my teeth. "Of course, who wouldn't want you to be their daughter-in-law?" I knew his mother hated her and wished he was with Emma, but my job was to keep everyone happy. "Think about it. If you have kids, you will have him by the balls for the rest of his life." She laughed. "You're so silly, Joaquin." I looked at her reaction, but she knew it as well and I knew she was a woman playing a game like everyone else. The sounds of stilettos were making their way down the hall and were getting closer.

Mike's mother emerged in a classic black and white Chanel suit with sunglasses to match. "Stephanie, where's my coffee? Please hurry. We don't want to miss our flight. I have to get back to my horses." "Sure thing, Mom." "Call me Mrs. Chapman, dear," she said as Stephanie walked into the kitchen. Mrs. Chapman pulled me aside. "Is my son treating you well?" I wanted to tell her that she raised a prick. "Yes, he is." "I wanted to talk to you about your acting. You really have to get on that." Stephanie returned and gave Mrs. Chapman her coffee. "Where's Joaquin's coffee?"

A visibly frustrated Stephanie returned to the kitchen. "Listen to me, I want you to be my eyes and ears here in Los Angeles with these two. I know Mike keeps a lot from me and I don't like Stephanie at all. If anything is going on between the two of them, I want you to update me. Whether by email or phone, you get in touch with me and keep me posted. Here are my details," she said as she handed me a card with her information. "Okay, I will Mrs. Chapman." Her sense of urgency and tone quickly changed as Stephanie walked in with my coffee. "You have to stay focused on your acting, Joaquin. You don't have anyone holding you back so make sure to follow through with your dreams. I fulfilled my career goals when I became a psychiatrist but after I became a mother, it fulfilled me in other ways, and I stopped working to focus on my children." She took off her sunglasses. "A woman has to be prepared to make those decisions when they become serious with someone. I was an independent woman who made sacrifices. Not a social climber who's only out for herself," she said as she looked at Stephanie. "Well, sometimes a woman can have it all," Stephanie said. "Oh, darling, don't be a fool," Mrs. Chapman said. Mrs. Chapman wanted her son to be happy and she was not going to let any woman stand in the way of that. She was also trying to freak out Stephanie so she would walk away from the relationship with Mike. Mr. Chapman made his way into the dining room. "Good morning." He was dressed as if he was going to play golf. He sat down and grabbed *The Los Angeles Times* off the table and sat down and began to lose himself in his reading. "He would like some coffee as well, Stephanie," Mrs. Chapman said. I looked at Stephanie as she retreated to the kitchen rolling her eyes at me. Only I noticed but it seemed as though she thought I was her ally in all of this. "Are we ready?" Mike said in a grumpy tone as he grabbed a piece of toast from the stack on the table and stuffed his mouth. "Have a little coffee, dear." "No, no, let's get moving. I have a busy day," he said. They all gathered their things. "Joaquin, get the bags from upstairs," Mike said. "Sure." "You go up and help him. They are your parents' bags." Mrs. Chapman snapped.

We both walked upstairs and when we arrived, Mike turned to me. "Good, now take all of the bags downstairs." "You wouldn't want your mother to know you didn't help me, would you?" He looked at me with angry piercing eyes. He grabbed two of the bags and we began our descent down the stairs. His mother apparently couldn't live without her Louis Vuitton collection of luggage. We arrived at the bottom of the staircase. His mother walked out of the kitchen. "I'm ready." "Mrs. Chapman, great luggage." "It was a gift dear from Marc when he was their designer." "Well, Mr. Jacobs treated you well." "Let's go already!" Mike shouted. Mike had already pulled the SUV out from the garage, so he had it parked in front of the house. As we exited the home, Rachael was standing in front of the house. "Rachael, so happy you could join us." Mrs. Chapman kissed and hugged Rachael. "Next time you have to stay longer so you can stay with me." "I know, dear, I'm sorry. We will. Maybe next time you'll be introducing me to your future husband." "I'm a lesbian, Mom." "Yes, I know dear, it was wishful thinking on my part." "Are you coming with us?" Mike asked. "No, I just stopped by to see them off," Rachael said. "Well, you did. Now go to the office. Those fucking employees get lazy if we are gone for too long." "Bye, Dad, have a great trip." She hugged her father in a long embrace. "Bye, sweetheart. You take care now and don't work too hard. Next time we come out, hopefully we will get to meet your special someone." "She has to have one first," Mike chimed in. "Okay, Dad, next time."

We all got into the SUV and Stephanie would soon be free from Mrs. Chapman. The ride to the airport was a silent one. A stark contrast from when we picked them up. This time, instead of getting to know each other, Mrs. Chapman knew all that she wanted to know about Stephanie. Stephanie was anxious to see Mike's parents off and was definitely glad that they lived in Florida. So much so that Stephanie made a donation to one of Mrs. Chapman's favorite charities. "Mrs. Chapman, I wanted to mention that I read more about the horse rescue that you support in West Palm Beach and I donated a thousand dollars." "Dear, true charity is not meant to be publicized but your effort and generosity with Mike's money is not only appreciated but noted." There was an awkward silence.

Once we arrived at LAX, Mike went to find a parking spot so we could all go in to say goodbye to his parents. If it were up to Stephanie, she would dump them curbside. Stephanie needed time to heal from the emotional wounds she endured from Mrs. Chapman. Mike parked the vehicle in long-term parking, and he actually helped me drag the luggage through the parking garage. "Stephanie, that one isn't too heavy, can you take that one?" Mrs. Chapman had to get one last request before she headed back to the sunshine state. "Of course, Mom." Mrs. Chapman rolled her eyes under her Chanel specs. We arrived at the terminal and to the security checkpoint, which for Stephanie may as well have been the gates of heaven on that day. We all said our goodbyes and his parents were on their way. Stephanie waved with tears of joy in her eyes as she blew kisses. His mother didn't look back once. His father turned around a few times to wave back. Mike just stood there and gave a simple wave. Once we couldn't see them anymore as they were swallowed by the crowds of people heading to their next destination, we turned around and made our way to the parking garage. "What a week," Stephanie said. "What the fuck is that supposed to mean?" He asked. I continued walking in silence pretending to ignore their exchange. "What is that supposed to mean? It wasn't an easy week. I was entertaining your parents all week while you were in the office for a great part of it. Your mother didn't make it a walk in the park." "Don't act like it was work." "Not work?! I might as well have been working. Spending time with your mother was a full-time job." They continued to bicker until we arrived at the house. "I'll see you at the office, Mike," I said. I stepped out and said goodbye to Stephanie, got in my car, and drove to the office.

Once I left, I could hear them continue their arguing. As I approached the office, I noticed crowds gathered outside of the doors. I thought something had happened, but it turned out it was a group of militant mothers (MAVVG- Mothers Against Violent Video Games) taking a stance against the *Homicide* franchise and Imperial itself. I paused for a second when I realized that I had to enter the building through the back where a security guard, who looked like a secret service agent, greeted me. I showed my ID and was let up through the freight elevator. I walked to my desk and could hear the demonstrators from the street. I checked my email and noticed an email from Charles Santos, our PR Director, instructing us not to look out any window to avoid being photographed by any photographers or press. The last thing any of the employees needed was to be identified by angry menopausal mothers.

Thirty minutes later, Mike walked into the office and I knew right then that this day was not going to get any better. The phones were ringing off the hook. I fielded calls all day from kids asking to speak to Mike. They thought he was the coolest guy, even though the games he created were intended for adults. Young boys would call the office asking to speak to him to tell him that his games were amazing and that they were huge fans. The loyal kids who somehow managed to fork over sixty dollars for video games and then whose parents were concerned about the violence in them. This, however, was not going to stop. The empire continued growing at a frantic pace. "Come into my office now." I quickly stood up from my desk and walked into his office. "Close the door, I need you to get my cable fixed immediately. Stephanie's out shopping and will be gone all day. I don't know what's wrong with it, I can't seem to get any of my channels." It just so happened that I had a friend who worked for Spectrum and was always able to get a tech to look at Mike's cable at his house at a moment's notice. I just had to throw him some cash, games, and T-shirts since he was a big fan of the *Homicide* series. Mike loved the fact I was able to get things done quickly and he came to expect that every time he made a request. He handed me the keys to his place. "Also, take the bitch home. I shouldn't have brought her in today with all those crazy cunts outside." Regan's head rose from where she was laying down and looked as though she did not want to move from her camouflage doggy bed and a decapitated cat's head toy. It looked like a prop from *The Texas Chainsaw Massacre*. I put Regan's leash on and being her stubborn self, she did not want to move. She threw herself on the ground. I picked her up and closed the office door behind me. I placed her on the ground, and she threw herself to the floor again. Luckily, in my spare time I watched enough *Dog Whisperer* episodes. I knew to shorten the leash and made the bitch walk. She quickly realized I wasn't going to play into her bullshit. I placed her in my car and had a special seatbelt Mike made me purchase, for my car, for Regan.

At Mike's house, I entered the gate code and quickly made my way into the house. Regan was very alert as she pulled me up the stairs. Surprisingly, she was not barking as she normally did. This time she just pulled and was eager to get upstairs. I made my way up the stairs to see what she sensed. I heard something coming from the master bedroom. No one should have been home, especially since Mike's parents left that morning, Stephanie was out shopping, and Lupita was at the office. I went into the bedroom and it was empty. The bed was left unmade, and Mike's clothes were on the floor. Nothing looked out of place. I realized the noise was coming from the screening room. He must have left a film playing because I could hear heavy moans and groans of a sex scene or porn. When I approached the slightly ajar door, I realized it was porn. Except it wasn't on the screen, it was Stephanie and Rachael on the plush chocolate sofa in an uncompromising position. To say they were scissor sisters was putting it mildly. They nearly blinded me with their pale bodies. I decided to take a few photos with my phone. As I did this, Regan began to bark because she wanted a piece of the action. I unhooked the leash. "Regan?" Stephanie said. I quickly moved away from the door as Regan ran into the screening room. "What are you doing here?" Stephanie asked Regan as if she was going to get an answer. "Fuck," Rachael said as she ran into the adjacent studio. I made my way downstairs quietly. "Hi, Stephanie, it's Joaquin. I didn't realize you were here," I said. "Oh, hi J. She walked down the stairs in her usual disheveled form. Tattered blue jeans, white V-neck T-shirt, messy hair and flip-flops. She's clearly at the comfortable stage of their relationship where she doesn't try as hard. "Regan woke me up from a nap." Regan ran down the stairs with an expression that read, "You lying bitch." She quickly ran back up the stairs barking, I'm sure to find Rachael. "Regan! Shut-up!" "I'm here to meet with the cable guy, he is coming to fix the issue you guys have with the reception." "I returned back early from shopping; I couldn't find much of anything." I spotted close to ten luxury shopping bags in the living room. "Go back to the office and let Mike know that I will take care of it." "Are you sure?" "Yes, definitely."

I walked out of the house and I saw a Spectrum van at the gate. I looked up at one of the windows and saw someone standing there watching me. As quickly as I looked, the curtain moved, and I headed back to the office. When I arrived at the office, Mike was surprised to see me. "What are you doing back so soon?" "Stephanie was home. She was already back from shopping and said she would wait for the cable guy." What I really wanted to say was, your girlfriend was making a fool out of you, you dumb fuck, but instead, I enjoyed watching how his dramatic personal life would play out. "Have you seen Rachael?" he asked. "Here at the office?" "Yes, never mind, there she is. Rachael, get in here." Rachael walked into his office looking just as disheveled as Stephanie had only twenty minutes prior. "Why the hell do you look like you just rolled out of bed? It's fucking 11:30am." "I had a rough night. I was getting a lot of writing done." I tried to listen to the conversation, but Rachael closed the door as soon as she entered the office. I watched them from the corner of my eye through the window. Mike pulled a baby blue box from his drawer. The distinct baby blue that could only be Tiffany & Co. He displayed it to Rachael, a small box containing a ring. This could only mean that he was going to ask Stephanie to marry him. I could tell that Rachael was trying to be happy for him but how could she when she was sleeping with Stephanie. Mike looked as though he was discussing a business transaction with Rachael instead of speaking about how he was about to ask Stephanie to marry him. Then again, he was marrying Stephanie. It was a business transaction with zero return on investment.

Mike placed the ring in a brown paper bag and threw it on his desk. The tone of their conversation quickly changed. Rachael exited the office and returned with two scripts in her hand. Mike grabbed one and looked it over. He immediately stood up and started yelling at Rachael as she was seated. Mike's face was tomato red and he began sweating because he was so pissed. He walked out of the office and came in my direction. "J, make a copy of this script my sister has yet to finish." He threw it on my desk and walked into his office without closing the door. He began screaming at Rachael. They exchanged words but Mike definitely had the last word. "I gave you a chance, this time, in writing the script instead of hiring a ghostwriter again so you can get the recognition you want, and you still can't get the fucking thing done you useless piece of shit." Rachael walked out with her ego crushed and with her head held down. She avoided eye contact with anyone as she was visibly embarrassed. I walked by Rachael's office on my way back from the copier and her shades were pulled down so she could be shrouded from prying eyes. It was too late; my eyes had seen enough of what I needed to see. She was protected from Mike, but she wasn't protected from me.

A few hours later I decided to call my friend Justin, from Spectrum, he was one of the few heterosexual male friends I had who never went through a sexual exploration phase with guys. He was all about the ladies, so we never had sex.

"Justin, can you do me a huge favor? Did your friend leave my boss's place yet?" "Yeah, he left about thirty minutes ago." "I need to meet up with him." "Okay, what for? He isn't gay." "I don't want to sleep with him, dickhead, I have some questions." "Alright, I am having drinks with Miguel at Crazy Girls tonight on LaBrea. Meet us there." "That's predictable." "We're straight, what do you expect?" I was going to be surrounded by Summer Eve cleansed, perfumed sprayed vaginas all while trying to find out some information regarding what happened at Mike's home after I left. I had to take one for the team, but it was going to be worth it.

CHAPTER 20

MONEY MOVES

I rushed home after work, and I took a shower. I grabbed a ton of singles I kept in the dresser from bartending and went to the ATM to withdraw five hundred dollars just in case. I walked into Crazy Girls at 9:00 p.m. I wanted to get in and out of there as quickly as possible. I often wondered why Justin would blow his money in this place. He was a marketing manager at Spectrum and at the age of thirty had not settled down with a single woman. He definitely dedicated time to sleeping around, but he just hadn't found the time or desire to be with just one woman. Having an affinity for strippers didn't help. I only hung out with him once or twice a year when he guilted me into hanging out with him, but we had nothing in common other than having worked together at Urban Outfitters when we were in college. He was having sex with a customer in the fitting rooms, and I covered for him when our boss was looking for him. Since, in his eyes, he felt we were bonded for life. At the moment, we were because I needed to ask Miguel what he saw when he went to Mike's house.

When I spotted them, they were seated in two lounge chairs with one stripper in Miguel's lap and the other in Justin's. I knew this was going to take some work to get Miguel's attention long enough to answer my questions. There were perfume infused scantily clad bodies everywhere. All of the women looked as though they drenched their bodies in baby oil to maintain a sleek sheen to their complexions. The dress code might as well be clothing optional for what little the women were wearing. One of the cocktail waitresses asked me. "Hi, sexy, can I get you something to drink?" "Yes, actually, can you tell me what my friends over there are drinking?" "They have been drinking Stella and also Casamigos shots." "Can you get me a Belvedere, club soda, and lime and two Stellas for them as well as three shots of Casamigos." "Okay baby, I'll bring it over to you." "Hey guys what's up?" I said as I walked over to them. "Yo J, what's up? I would stand but as you can see, I'm busy. Miguel, this is Joaquin, you went to his boss's house today." "Oh, word, what's up?" he said while his eyes were fixated on the Brazilian stripper's tits in front of him. I knew this wasn't going to be easy, but I pulled a seat right next to Miguel. "Ooh, a threesome," the stripper said. "No, not a threesome," he said to the stripper and quickly turned to me. "Stop cock blockin' bro, she's mine." "I don't mind sharing," the stripper said. "I don't share," Miguel said. "Bro, what do you want? You see, I'm busy." The waitress arrived with the drinks I'd ordered and handed them their third round and my first. "The drinks are on your cute friend here," the waitress said as she placed the drinks down and winked at me. "Thanks bro," the guys said in unison. Justin took his drink into the Champagne Room to spend all his money on a stripper.

Miguel looked in envy while keeping his eye on his Brazilian prize. He couldn't afford the Champagne Room. "Miguel, I want to know if you saw anything out of the ordinary at my boss's place?" "Nah, I was there for an hour and a half and

I did the job and left." "Who was at the house at the time?"
"Look, I'll answer your questions if you give me money to go
to the Champagne Room with Candela here." "How much
do you want?" "Five hundred dollars?" "You want to spend
five hundred dollars on a stripper who isn't going to fuck
you?" "Fuck you, bro. You want information, right?' "Fine,
I'll pay for your blue balls." "Candela, warm up that Champagne Room, baby, I'm coming for you." "Who was at the
house when you arrived?" I asked Miguel as Candela walked
away shaking her ass. "A snooty bitch and another woman
in a suit." "Did they say anything?" "To me, no, but when I
was checking on the box in the screening room, I overheard
her saying that she was pregnant, but Mike didn't know yet."
"Really, are you sure?" I had my doubts since he was on his
third round. The other woman was definitely shocked and
upset at the same time. They tried to whisper but I heard everything. She kept saying that she had to leave Mike and that
she wanted to be with the woman. It sounded like straight
up novela in that fuckin' house. Like a *General Hospital* episode. Those chicks are definitely fucking." "What do you
know about *General Hospital*?" I asked. "My mom loves that
shit." Anyway, the other woman's phone started ringin' off
the chain. She said that Mike was lookin' for her and that she
had to go back to the office. The last thing she said was that
she would take care of matters and that everything would
work out. That's all I know. Now give me my fuckin' money
so I can have Candela's tetas all to myself."

I handed him the five hundred dollars and he headed off to
Rio de Janeiro. At least for the night. I checked the time and
noticed that I had been there for only forty-five minutes. I
finished my drink and made my way out. As I walked out the
waitress stopped me. "Hey, baby, are you leaving soon?" "Yes,
I have to get home to my wife." "All the guys in here have to
get home to their wives but they are still here." "Yeah, well I
am married to a Puerto Rican woman so if I don't get home,

I won't have a home to go to." She laughed, "Oh, you're Puerto Rican too." "Yes, so you know I have to get out of here," I said with laughter. Have a good night." I walked out of Crazy Girls with less money than I walked in with but extremely rich with information. Mission Accomplished.

CHAPTER 21

THE PROPOSAL

The following day, Mike asked me to make reservations at Perch for 8:00 p.m. He was getting ready to propose to Stephanie in the most romantic way he could, but he wasn't good at this sort of thing. All day he was incredibly frustrated and on edge. He might have had second thoughts, but he must have believed this was what he was supposed to do in the grand scheme of things. Work, marry, and breed. I made the reservations. Immediately after I got off the phone with the restaurant, Stephanie walked into the office. It was probably because she could smell the diamond all the way from home. She looked like something was definitely bothering her. It was probably that she was about to gain weight with her meal ticket, I mean first child on the way. She had Regan in tow who was definitely not keen on sharing Mike with Stephanie and was very difficult with her. "Regan, come on," Stephanie tugged. She walked right into Mike's office. "What are you doing here? I thought we weren't going to see each other until tonight?" "Yeah, I know but there is something I want to talk to you about." "Well, save it for tonight. I'm busy." Mike continued to look at his computer screen. "Alright, that's fine.

I'm leaving Regan here." "Leave her with J." he said as Stephanie walked out and deposited Regan at my desk. "Here is Regan. She is stressing me out again and I definitely don't need that today. I'm so exhausted." "Oh, no worries. I'll bring her home later." "Thanks, you're a lifesaver."

That evening, as they prepared to leave for dinner, I arrived at his home with Regan. "J, do me a favor and stay here until I return. Watch the beast for me. She's been chewing on my fucking furniture and I hate to crate her." I wasn't expecting to spend my Thursday night babysitting Regan, but I could catch up on some Netflix. He had on a jacket and slacks, as dressy as he could possibly be. He wanted to show Stephanie that he was making an effort. She had on a black Dior dress with silver Louboutin pumps. The minute they left I threw myself on the sofa in the screening room and of course Regan followed and had to lay on me. For some reason, she loved me. I was the only person that didn't take her shit and she respected me. I decided to watch *The Texas Chainsaw Massacre*. An eerie cinematic experience when you have the kind of screening room Mike had. I felt like I was hiding in a room from Leatherface, but I loved it. Regan would growl when he would come on screen. She didn't like anyone in a mask. That might be why she didn't like Stephanie.

An hour and a half passed and as Marilyn screamed for her life in the ending of the film, I heard the downstairs door slam and Regan began barking. I shut the film off and made my way downstairs. "Is everything alright?" "No, everything is not alright. It's a fucking disaster. Stephanie just told me she is fucking pregnant. I don't know how that is fucking possible. I smoke so much weed, I didn't think I could get her pregnant." I stood there staring at him in disbelief of what I just heard him say. He was a shrewd businessman but in his personal life he could be ignorant. "Well, women do become pregnant despite their men smoking weed. Especially if they aren't using protection themselves." "I always pull-out before I cum. One of those fuckers must have gotten through. Fuck!" "What happened after she told you?" "I threw the ring I had at her and said 'Here' and thanked her for ruining my surprise." "You were proposing?" "I did. I gave her the ring. I was ready to give her a ring, but I wasn't ready to become a father." "Where is she?" "She went to stay with one of her model friends who's in town. J, get out of here. That will be all for tonight." I didn't waste any time making my way out of his place. "Wait." Just when I thought I was free, he of course had another request. "Turn on the firepit and then you can go. I'm going upstairs to take a bath." He always hated taking showers and preferred taking baths, which I found weird. He was always on edge, a bath seemed so tranquil for him. He was probably plotting on who at the office he was going to fire next. With the fire roaring I closed the door behind me and locked it. I drove home and looked at my phone and realized it was already 10:30 p.m. When I arrived home, I threw myself on my bed and passed out.

CHAPTER 22

BANG BANG

The following day, I woke up groggy and peeled myself out of bed. I could have kept sleeping after Mike's emotional outburst last night drained me. I think I was more emotionally drained than he was. I turned the TV on to *Good Morning America* and headed into the bathroom. As I brushed my teeth, I could hear Robin Roberts greeting me as she did every morning with breaking news. "Violent video games have become a reality for Mike Chapman, the president and founder of Imperial Games as he was murdered on the grounds of his Beverly Hills estate last night. He suffered multiple gunshot wounds and the suspect is still at large." I spit my toothpaste out and sprinted the short distance to my TV. I felt that I was in the midst of a nightmare. I was seeing the reporter's mouth move but I wasn't hearing anything. I was in complete shock. I didn't have time to take it all in before there was a knock on my door. I had to put a towel on. "Who is it?" "Beverly Hills PD, please open the door." I looked through the peephole and noticed there were two detectives outside of my door. I opened it. "Are you Joaquin Otero?" "Yes, I am." "I'm Detective Michaels and this is Detective Johnson. We are going to need you to come to the station to answer questions about your boss, Mike Chapman. Are you aware that he was murdered last night?" "I just heard it on TV." "Okay, we will wait right here." "I will get dressed."

The two detectives escorted me out of my building. I felt as though I was wanted for something. I was hoping none of my neighbors witnessed this, so they didn't think I was some sort of criminal. When we got to the lobby, I saw Mrs. Wilson, the nosey cat lady who was always watching the coming and goings of my building. She pulled her glasses down and went back into her apartment. When we were outside, the more attractive of the two officers opened the back door of their car and I got in. They drove me to the precinct where everyone and anyone who knew Mike was sure to be questioned. I was numb. I couldn't believe what was happening all at the same time, I kept thinking of the times when I purchased drugs for Mike or handled his prostitution transactions. I am sure all of this was going to come up or I was going to be charged with committing a crime. We stepped out of the vehicle and went into the police station that reminded me of a *Law & Order* episode. They walked me into a room with a cold metal table and offered me some coffee. I sat down and waited to be questioned. A man in a gray suit that looked about two sizes too small walked into the room carrying a legal pad. "Mr. Otero, my name is Detective O'Sullivan. I want to ask you some questions regarding your relationship with Mr. Chapman. What did you do for Mr. Chapman?" "I was his personal assistant." "What did that entail exactly?" "The short answer, managing his entire life." "And the long answer?" "Calendar management, restaurant reservations, travel arrangements, internal correspondence and personal arrangements." "What kind of personal things?" "Grocery shopping, meeting with repairmen, the cleaning lady, personal trainer and general shopping." "Anything else?" I felt like maybe he already knew about Shana and that was what he was getting at or maybe he knew about Romalice. "There was a large stash of drugs in Mr. Chapman's home. He served time for having drugs in his possession in the past and we suspect they were purchased from Romalice Williams, a notorious drug dealer in DTLA who was almost killed during a raid. When he was arrested, we questioned him regarding his connection to Mike Chapman but, he denied that Mr. Chapman was a client of his. However, when we seized his possessions, he had every Imperial video game, the game consoles and company merchandise. I'm betting he didn't buy them." "Or maybe he stole them," I said. "Maybe your boss gave them to him." "I don't know." Except I did know that Brenda had given all of those games and the systems to Romalice before I had started working at Imperial. She did that because Romalice would always give Mike extras and Mike wanted to make sure that he was taken care of in return. "Any idea where the Cocaine came from?" "Colombia?", I said. "Don't be a smart-ass Mr. Otero, have you ever met this Romalice?" "No, I can't say that I have." "Are you sure?" "I'm sure, I don't know who Romalice is." "We also stopped by Hancock Park, Mr. Chapman's old neighborhood, and spoke to a few neighbors to see if they had seen anyone that frequented Mr. Chapman's old house. One neighbor in particular stated that a has-been model who worked for him, the young man with the attitude, and then she also mentioned that a young woman who she assumed was a prostitute frequently visited Mr. Chapman's home. Would you know who she is referring to?" "Shana?" "Yes, Shana Roberts. Ms. Roberts, whose real name is Lizbeth Collins, stated that Mr. Chapman was a regular client but abruptly stopped. She doesn't recall when. She was cooperative and we didn't press any charges against her." Detective O'Sullivan stood up, pushing back his chair in frustration and got in my face. "It is in your best interest to cooperate with me."

At that moment, another detective walked into the interrogation room. "We are done with questioning here. Witnesses from last night said they saw an African American male flee the property. We have camera footage from one of the neighboring homes." I recognized the detective because it was the same one who stopped me at Romalice's building. I used my acting skills on him when he stopped me for questioning that day. I thought I was going to be caught for lying. "Do I know you from somewhere?" he asked. "No, not that I'm aware of?" He walked out with a puzzled look. "Okay, you are free to go, if we have further questions, we will contact you." "Not a problem." I walked out of the precinct and was still numb from the news that Mike was gone. In my rush to get dressed, I didn't have either of my phones on me, so I had no idea if anyone had been trying to reach me. I got to my apartment and I had 50 missed calls in total, and my voicemail was full. "OMG J! Call me! I'm a wreck!" Stephanie. "J, did you hear about it? Call me." Brenda. "J, give me a call when you get this." Rachael. "Mijo, ay dios mío llámame!" Lupita. I listened to the first six messages of everyone telling me to give them a call and I just had to sit down for a minute. I didn't want to talk to anyone. I turned the TV on and the lead story on the news was that the authorities were looking for a male suspect caught on camera fleeing from the scene of the crime. Apparently after I left, Mike had decided to do laps in the pool. No one heard anything because the assailant had used a silencer. Still in shock, I made my way to the office mid-day. I had no idea what to expect. I wasn't sure if I was going to walk into a building with people relieved that Mike was gunned down or that they would be mourning him as they would a loved one.

When the elevator doors opened to the office, the mood was definitely somber. The faces of the employees looked lost. They didn't know what to do with themselves. Their leader was gone. None of the executives had arrived yet. I sat at my desk and turned on my computer. I looked at Mike's office through the glass. All of a sudden, an overweight tester appeared in front of me. "I don't know what to do with myself. This is crazy." He looked to me for guidance, but I was the wrong person. If it were up to me, I would put him on a diet and send him to the gym, but I had to do my best under the circumstances. "I think the best thing to do is work through the day until midnight. It would have meant a lot to Mike to show your dedication," I said. In honor of Mike, I decided to be a prick. I took forty dollars out of petty cash. "Here, order yourself a pizza." His eyes lit up. "Thanks." He walked back to his desk like a robot in typical Imperial fashion. "Fat fuck," I said under my breath. I went online to get a sense of what the news outlets were saying on the web. My phone began to ring. "Hello." "Hi J, Oh my God." "Brenda?" "I'm in St. Barths, I had to get out of Cali. Not to be a bitch but even when I'm trying to relax Mike has to interfere with my happiness. I'm with a hot twenty-five-year-old guy. Christ, what was I doing married all of those years?" "Where is your baby?" I asked. "My husband has full custody, but I still get alimony from the son of a bitch. I can't believe his band actually made it but I'm happy they did. Look at me now. Excuse me, can I get another piña colada please? Ugh, they are so slow here. Do they know who did it?" "They believe it was a young black guy, a crazed fan of the games. They are searching for him but right now, that's all I know." "A black guy, surprise, surprise," she said as she slurped her drink. How is his girlfriend?" She asked. "Not sure, I haven't spoken to her." Then in a quieter voice, I filled her in. "The night before this happened, she told Mike that she was pregnant, and he was proposing to her and threw the ring at her when he found out." "What a piece of work, she stepped in shit. She didn't need to get a ring to get those checks coming in. I bet she doesn't miss him at all," Brenda said. "Brenda, I'm happy to hear from you and hang in there. Stay strong and be in touch." I could hear her gulping her drink as she came up for air. "Ok, I will." What I really wanted to say was, have another drink and fuck off. But I was an actor. A struggling, out of work one, but an actor, nonetheless.

Calls began pouring in as soon as I hung up with Brenda. Everyone from reporters, fans and acquaintances. I was getting so many calls that I had to send them to voicemail. At 5:00 p.m., Rachael walked into the office. Instead of walking into her office, she walked into Mike's, sat down and signaled for me to come in. "J, I need food. Can you go to Shake Shack and get me a burger, fries and a large Diet Coke." "Sure," I said as I waited for her to give me cash. "Do you need cash? Didn't Mike have petty cash?" "Yes, I said." "Take it out of there." "Did the detectives have any more information?" I asked. "Apparently, they think that the person who did this is some crazed fan or potentially a protester of our games. He's a fucking piece of shit." I just stood there staring at her in silence and couldn't help but to think that there was no emotion coming through those words. "Sick bastard," she said, finally choking up a bit. I still didn't buy it. "J, I need to be alone." "Ok, no worries," I said as I walked out of the office to grab her early dinner. I went to Shake Shack and I couldn't help but think that Rachael was already making plans to renovate Mike's office and make it hers. I didn't understand why a fan would want to kill off Mike. If anything, they would want to kill off the protestors one by one. However, in this day and age with everyone wanting their fifteen minutes of fame, people would do anything. "J, I'm going to need you to write a speech, to everyone internally, so I can address them in the morning. Get started on it now and I'll edit it." I sat at my desk, writing until about 10:00 p.m. and kept pausing to read updates online and on social media. I was drained by it all. I headed home to drown myself in bottles of wine.

When I arrived, I threw my things on the floor and realized I had voicemail messages on my phone. I didn't want to listen to all of them. It was Lupita. I opened a bottle of wine and began drinking. "Joaquín! Soy yo, Lupita. Te tengo que hablar." She sounded anxious. My phone began ringing. "Joaquín, hola mijo." She sounded out of breath as I was almost done with glass number one and poured my second. "Lupita, dónde estás?" I heard a knock at my door. I opened it and it was Lupita, completely out of breath. You would have thought she just climbed Everest. She charged inside of my apartment. "Lupita, que haces aquí? Es tarde." "Dame agua." I grabbed a bottle of water out of the fridge and handed it to her after asking what she was doing at my place so late. I waited as she gulped it down.

She finished the entire sixteen- ounce bottle without saying a word. "Mijo, tengo algo que decirte," she said as she began to calm down. "¿Qué pasa? Yo se de Mike. Si yo estaba en la casa de Rachael anoche, antes qué pasó todo." She went on to tell me that she was cleaning Rachael's apartment last night and that she overheard her telling someone on the phone not to worry. Then she told this person that she loved them before hanging up. "Ella estaba hablando con Stephanie." "¿Cómo lo sabes?" She didn't tell me anything I didn't already know. She continued to tell me she was cleaning Rachael's home office the day before Mike was killed. Rachael was in the kitchen on the phone and Lupita accidently pressed the speaker button. I wasn't sure how much of an accident it actually was but when she rushed to turn it off, she lowered the volume. "Stephanie está embarazada." She shared something else I already knew, but I pretended to be in shock. However, she said Rachael also mentioned that everything was going to be fine and that Mike's death would not be tracked back to her. I stood frozen. I couldn't believe what Lupita had discovered. She was frantic and continued to clean the apartment as if she hadn't heard a thing. She then drove over to my apartment to inform me of what was going on.

I turned on the news to see if there was any further development and they showed surveillance video of the young guy running from Mike's house. The police were after this guy, searching for his whereabouts. Now I knew the monster was much larger than a young thug who would become infamous for taking out the godfather of gaming. An African American thug was not a common sight in Beverly Hills. The next morning, Rachael was already in her office when I arrived. I handed her the speech as she skimmed it and made a few minor changes. "Round up everyone in the office near the marketing department in an hour." I sent an email out immediately. An hour later, we all gathered near the marketing department area of the office and waited for Rachael. She walked over appearing strong and somber. "As you all know, this is a very difficult time for me and my family. I appreciate that you have all continued to work full steam ahead because that is what Mike would have wanted. We have a lot of important titles in the pipeline that can't be sidelined by these unfortunate events. I will take over the role as president." Her emotion was so fake that not even a ghetto bitch would have purchased it in Chinatown. I could see the darkness in her eyes simultaneously with the gleam of her future that would catapult her into the spotlight. Everyone would look to her for the answers and her parents would finally lean on her instead of Mike. The pride they had for Mike would shift to her. "We have to stick together, as the family we are." Although Rachael was the Chief Creative Officer and could write scripted street dialogue and choppy slang, she would have the research department make sure that she was always accurate. She did not have a way with words. Eloquent, she was not. After she finished speaking, everyone clapped to show their support for her and the "family." I was not as enthusiastic.

Several days passed and still no leads in the case. I found it surprising how the suspect could elude officers for so many days. Three weeks later, Rachael received a visit from the BHPD, at the office, notifying her that the suspect, Jamal Johnson, was found and that he had committed suicide by hanging himself. The officers found press clippings, about Imperial and specifically about Mike, at the suspect's apartment and all of Imperial's games. There were also photographs of Mike. The suspect left a suicide note detailing that he had killed Mike in order to become famous and also because he was an aspiring game designer and had sent Mike proposals regarding his game ideas, but they went unanswered. There were also some calls to Mike's office line on his phone records. The suspect felt ignored and disrespected. This was his way of rebelling and taking *Homicide* to the next level. The 57-caliber pistol used in the crime was not found in the apartment. The officers suggested to Rachael that she or other employees could be potential targets in the future so heightened security at the office should be considered. Rachael listened to what the detectives told her, but it went in one ear and out the other. The Chapmans always cherished privacy over safety. Having security guards around in the office all of the time would mean that there would be eyes watching every move. This was not something that would be welcomed at all nor would it be implemented. One monster dies and another is born. Imperial had a new leader who didn't play by the rules.

CHAPTER 23

THE FUNERAL

The funeral wasn't a private affair at all. It took place at Pierce Brothers in Westwood Village and was a virtual who's who of the fashion world. Not because Mike actually knew these people, but because Stephanie did. This was turning out to be a fashion event rather than a memorial service for the titan of gaming. It was a sea of couture and designer suits. The only thing missing was Anna Wintour, but she doesn't do video games. Stephanie was draped in black head-to-toe Dior.

When Mike's parents arrived at the chapel his mother, who was in black Chanel, walked over to Stephanie and wiped a tear from her cheek with a silk handkerchief. She hugged Stephanie. "I don't believe your emotions for one second, you gold-digging whore." Mrs. Chapman backed away and gave Stephanie an emotional grimace as if those words didn't come out of her mouth. Stephanie's look of shock conveyed that she couldn't believe what Mrs. Chapman said to her. Tears ran down her face, but I couldn't tell if she was crying because of Mike or crying about what was said to her. Mr. Chapman was very reserved and consoled his wife, but his eyes weren't even watery. If this was a Latino family, the mother would have been overcome with grief screaming for God to help and emotions would be far more apparent than the sea of ghosts who were in attendance. They made more of an effort to get dressed up than to even waste an ounce of emotion on Mike. Rachael sat with her parents in a tailored black on black Tom Ford suit. Her eyes were dead set on the casket and said more than her body language could. They were more rested than they were in recent days and conveyed that she was somewhat relieved that she would no longer be compared to her older brother. She no longer resided in his shadow. I sat in the front and turned around for a moment. In the back I could see red locks that looked so familiar. I looked again and they belonged to a very tanned Brenda. She stood there with her new boy toy and winked at me. I looked at Stephanie again and runny mascara covered her cheeks as the downpour of tears continued, all the way to the bank. Mike's presence wasn't gone, it was simply transferred to Rachael. I knew she wouldn't get rid of me even though, employees were dropping like flies because they believed with Mike gone, there was no future.

Once the funeral service was over, the reception was held at Mike's home. There was a spread of pastries, coffee and tea. There was a huge headshot of Mike. Every time I walked by it, I felt as though his eyes were moving and following me. It was kind of creepy. I noticed Brenda wasn't there. This gathering was much more private than the funeral itself. I helped usher people into Mike's screening room, where a short documentary paying tribute to Mike was displayed on the screen. One of the employees was up all night putting this together and while doing so was probably thinking what a prick Mike was. The short film contained footage of Mike from his childhood through his days at Pavement Films in Miami and his early days invading Los Angeles. Rachael did the voiceover narration and spoke about how she looked up to her brother and how as a child always wanted to be like him. I didn't think that ever ended. Mike's mother was crying on Rachael's shoulder and I took a glimpse at Stephanie and I noticed she rolled her eyes after realizing she wasn't a part of this documentary. She was a speck that Mrs. Chapman would like to forget.

After the film was over, Mrs. Chapman gathered herself to say a few words. "I want to thank you all for being here for showing support for my son and family. We are eternally grateful. Mike left behind a mother, father, sister, and dog, precious Regan, who loved him very much and we will always miss him. His legacy will remain in the company he built to entertain everyone, which was his passion. Thank you." When Mrs. Chapman finished her speech, Stephanie calmly stood up and walked out straight to the pastry tray in the adjoining room. Five minutes later, Mrs. Chapman appeared behind her. "You shouldn't eat too many of those, my dear. You don't have the type of body that can recover from that kind of indulgence." Stephanie turned around. "It's okay, I'm eating for two." "What? You mean that isn't emotional weight?" "No, I'm pregnant with Mike's child." "Don't think that you are going to get Mike's money just because that child is his. That trick may have worked for your mother, but you have me to deal with, my dear. Also, I expect you to vacate Mike's home immediately. It's his home after all, not yours. You aren't a widow." Mrs. Chapman put her sunglasses on and walked towards Mr. Chapman as everyone began spilling out of the screening room. I looked at all of the attendees and realized none of them were Mike's friends. Many of them paid their respects to Stephanie before leaving and expressed their remorse without obvious compassion. For them, it was just another excuse to put on new designer clothes. For Rachael, it established her authority as the new leader. The question remained as to whether she was up to the task.

CHAPTER 24

WHEN THINGS FALL APART

The weeks following the funeral, I noticed that each time I walked into the office I'd be surprised to see how much light was coming in through the windows. The employees that remained actually had smiles on their faces and seemed much more relaxed. Then Rachael walked in. She had returned from Florida after burying Mike and giving her parents emotional support. "Joaquin, here take care of this." She flung a leash that was still attached to Regan. Rachael was never an animal lover and she showed it as she dismissed Regan into my desk area. "That thing was barking all fucking night. I want you to take it to a fucking shelter. One of those kill shelters." "She probably misses Mike, I'll take her if you don't want her," I said. "I don't give a fuck what this dog is going through. I am going through enough and I have a company to run so you can have her. Joaquin, first thing on your agenda, I want you to clear out this office and box my brother's things. Put them in storage and move my things in." Mike was just buried, and Rachael was ready to officially claim Mike's office. His office had been recently organized but Rachael was a notorious hoarder just as Mike was, so this was going to be another long and tedious process.

It took me three days to get everything out of Mike's office and into his empty storage closet. I began deciphering the mess that was in Rachael's office. Loose papers blanketing the floor. It was a sea of dead trees. I continued until everything was moved into her new office. For the next few months, Rachael got through her "mourning period" without a hitch. She had convinced her parents that it would be best to bury Mike back in Florida, so the week after the services in Los Angeles, Rachael returned to Florida to handle the burial there. Mrs. Chapman advised that she didn't want Stephanie to come because she already had the opportunity to mourn Mike in front of her friends. Once Mike was buried in Florida, Rachael was ready to take over Los Angeles. She was pleased to have Mike's body buried in Florida because she wanted to have it as far away as possible. Mike could no longer cast a shadow on her, even in death. Mike loved Los Angeles so much because it was the city where he made a name for himself and where his career exploded. Now it was Rachael's turn. She no longer had to envy Mike because she was now Mike. She appointed herself as the sitting President of Imperial Games until she could convince Jake Taylor that she should be the acting President. She wasn't the founder, but she was a Chapman after all.

The board at Tower Studios, however, wasn't at ease with Rachael immediately taking charge. They had faith in Mike to churn out the greatest titles and make them richer. However, they saw Rachael as a liability. Not to mention, Mike was a man. They weren't ready for a woman to take over the company regardless of how butch she could be. Mike's emotional little sister who sought attention and acclaim for herself instead of what was right for the company. They believed what she needed was a therapist, not power. Jake had to reassure the board that Rachael would do an excellent job and maintain the same stringent standards that Mike was famous for.

There was a mass exodus of employees. Even August, Annabel and Gavin all left. They were Mike's "friends" not Rachael's. They also saw this as their chance to be free. With Mike's death, they felt the company was dead as well. Rachael attempted to re-vamp Imperial as much as she could. There was a lot of gossip going around and Rachael was fed up with not being taken seriously. She began firing people and replacing them with her own friends. One of them was an overweight hipster who looked as though Rachael plucked him from Silverlake. Another was an effeminate, gay, slim French guy who was Rachael's college roommate. Rachael was doing everything in her power to keep the company moving forward with the same momentum as Mike did. She wanted to prove to everyone and herself that she was capable of running the empire. With all the changes at the company, this also meant that I would become Rachael's assistant. I knew she didn't realize that I was a loaded gun of information. After things settled down with all the changes that Rachael made, the only original employees that remained were me and Christina. She was a workaholic and good at her job, so Rachael kept her around. She knew she was an asset and that replacing her would cost more money. As things were in transition, I enjoyed my weekends. Mike had often contacted me and asked for things over the weekends, but since his death it seemed like I partially had my life back.

On a Monday morning, Rachael arrived in the office. "Here you go." She threw a large document on my desk. It looked familiar except it was entitled The Bible According to Rachael. "I know you're familiar with the way Mike liked things done but I like things done differently. I revised it over the weekend." I didn't say a word. Her demands were more insane than Mike's. It was her way of outdoing him. I placed it aside to be shredded. Four hours later, Rachael stepped out of her office. "I'm going for a walk." I checked the Internet for daily news reports. The headlines were "Killer Found in Video Game Murder," "Suicide Gamer," "Case Closed for *Homicide* Founder," and "Game Over: Killer Found." I noticed that the neighborhood where the killer resided was one of L.A.'s roughest. It was also one of the neighborhoods the researchers visited along with Rachael to take photos and video of their surroundings for *Homicide III*. This young man killing himself wouldn't be major news if he hadn't killed Mike. It would have been just another kid taking out the trash. In this case, himself. One less thug the world had to contend with.

The neighborhood where he lived wasn't safe, so I knew I had to visit during the day rather than the evening. There was a park near the apartment building where the murderer was found. People congregated and watched the basketball players duke it out. Instead of watching the game, I watched the street. I noticed a woman sitting near her window on the ground level of the apartment building where Mike's murderer lived. Locals seemed to greet her as they walked by. She appeared to know everyone. She looked like a roughed up, ghetto version of Maya Angelou, except she appeared to have been in her fair share of Vaseline layered fights back in her day. Her face was scarred and was definitely not a charm school graduate. I knew this was going to cost me. Luckily, before I left the office, I removed some cash from Mike's petty cash envelope. The remaining one thousand dollars. He was no longer going to need it. I walked up the stairs to the building and she stared at me like a hawk stalking its prey.

"Who are you here to see? I've never seen you before." "My name is Julio; I was hoping I could speak to you." "You a cop?" "No, I'm not." "I didn't think so, you sound bougie as hell." I couldn't help but laugh. "No, I'm a detective. Much more sophisticated than your regular officer." "You look too young to be a detective." "I age well." "Let me see your badge." Imperial kept replicas of a variety of lawful and unlawful items for promotional reasons. We had LAPD badges that were exact replicas except they said Imperial City on them. Unless she looked very closely, she wouldn't be able to notice that. She gazed at it from her window and didn't challenge me further. "I wanted to know if you saw anything suspicious with the young man in 3C?" "Why are you asking me questions? The police barely questioned me. They asked me if I saw something, I said no and they took that boy's body, no more questions asked. To them it was another cockroach they ain't have to deal with." "I'm just investigating a much larger case and was curious about the young man. Can I please come in?" I reached into my pocket and discretely pulled out $200 dollars and flashed it to her. "I still ain't see nothing." "Maybe $500 dollars?" She buzzed me in. I walked into her apartment and felt like I was transported to the seventies. The rooms were poorly lit and covered in wallpaper that had seen better days. "You can have a seat." She pointed to her '50s diner kitchen table that was draped in bills. I took a seat and she sat in front of me. "Can I have my money?" I handed her $500 dollars and she put it in her bra. I couldn't tell if she was wearing one because her breasts looked like they were sagging to her knees with the dress she had on. "Look at that, Jesus blessed me with fifty percent of my eyesight, but only fifty." "Ok, I'm giving you $500 more dollars more for 100 percent of your eyesight but that's all I have. You know Jesus helped people when they needed help." She stared at me like she was going to slap me. "My name ain't Jesus, hell it ain't even Mary and in this neighborhood, you have to help yourself. I have a stack of bills and this isn't Jerusalem. This is South Central." I placed $500 dollars on the table. "It's a miracle. I can see, I can see. Praise the Lord," she said as she snatched the money from the table and stuffed it in her sagging bra.

"I see everybody that comes into this building day and night. I'm always watching when people don't know I'm watching. That night, when they said Jamal took his life to the other side, I remember hearing a door slam hard when they came into the building. Everybody who lives in this bitch knows you don't be slamming doors because then you gotta deal with me. That door has been broken for the longest time and that fucking landlord doesn't fix shit in this muthafucka." "Did you see anyone? "I'm gettin' to that. You damn kids are so impatient these days. Respect your elders. So that noise had me jump out of my chair. See I was up watchin' *The Honeymooners*. I went to the window so I could go off on somebody. I knew that one of the kid's friends must have come in not realizing not to have the door slam. He didn't have many friends, but he had a couple who liked to test my patience.

When I heard somebody coming down the stairs, I was ready to shout at the bastard. When I looked, it wasn't one of his two friends. It was a tall guy with a black hoodie on, but his hands were pale as a ghost." "Was he white?" I asked. "Damn right he was white, shit. Ain't no white man be showing up in this building or this neighborhood for no damn reason unless it's the cops. Hell, our mailman ain't even white." "Did you notice anything special about the hoodie he had on?" "Well, I did notice a red 'I' on the right sleeve." I was wearing a similar hoodie under my jacket. "Like this one?" "Exactly like that one." "Did you see his face?" "He must have felt he was being watched because he turned around to look at the building and I moved away from my window. At that point I could have sworn it was a girl." I pulled out my phone and showed her a picture from Rachael and Mike at the Chateau. "Was this her?" She gazed at the photo and with excitement stood up from her chair. "Yup, that's the bitch. Damn, I thought it was a man. She got a pretty face though. "The officers didn't question you at all?" "I told them I ain't see nothing." "Okay, this is all I need. You have been very helpful. I appreciate you keeping our meeting to yourself."

"I've never seen you before in my life and you were never here. I also know you ain't a real detective, but I don't give a shit." I smiled. "You have a good evening and pay those bills." "Make sure you don't slam that door." I walked out of the building and into the darkness of the early evening and rushed back. This is South Central for fuck's sake. I drove quickly and absorbed everything I learned. Rachael must have hired Jamal to kill Mike and then she ended up killing Jamal and staged his apartment to make it appear that he killed himself. I went to work early the next day. I walked in and Rachael was in earlier than normal with the shades pulled down and the door closed. I noticed I had voicemail messages to check but I decided to check who Rachael was speaking to. I pressed the button to his line. "We can't let anyone find out that you and I are together right now." "I know that," Stephanie said. "Don't worry, everything is going to work out." I quietly hung up the phone and Rachael emerged a few seconds later. "Clear my schedule for the rest of the day." "You don't have any meetings scheduled." "Well, I'm stepping out, I won't be back for the remainder of the day." I was happy to see her go. I was wondering what would prompt her to take the day off like that. I knew it was time for me to schedule a meeting of my own. I grabbed my phone and began texting.

Hi, Jake, Are you still in town?

Yes, I am.

Can you meet me at Plummer Park in WeHo at 12:30 p.m. on the benches?

I'm having lunch with my wife and kids today in Beverly Hills. They are in town from New York.

Please reschedule that. You'll want to meet with me.

I'll see you at 12:30 p.m.

I sat down on one of the benches as I spotted Jake walking towards me. He sat down next to me and continued to look straight ahead with his sunglasses on. "Okay, what do you want? And make it quick." "I know you couldn't speak to me at Mike's funeral because you were with your wife, so I wanted to meet now." "I want to give you what you want, and I want us both to go our separate ways." "Now that Rachael has taken over, what is Tower going to do with Imperial?" "I have a serious offer to sell Tower to Adrenaline Games and I am moving forward with it, that's why I'm still in town. They would then have complete control over Imperial and Rachael wouldn't have the control that Mike did because she's not Mike. I'm tired of getting shit from everyone on the board, and honestly, I don't need to be in this business anymore. I don't need the money. The point is I am ready to walk away. Rachael cares more about attention than the business itself. Mike was all about the business. He would eat, breathe, drink, snort and smoke Imperial. Rachael can't be taken seriously. The board is letting her mourn but they are putting pressure on me and I'm exhausted."

"Do you take me seriously?" "Stop playing games with me Joaquin, what do you want?" "I want twenty-five million dollars." "Twenty-five million dollars, are you fucking crazy, who are you?" "I think that's a bargain for silence for what happened between us. Actually, come to think of it, you are a billionaire. Make it fifty million and I will completely disappear. You will sell Tower and both of us can go on living our lives as if our paths never crossed." He remained silent and kept looking straight ahead. I could see the concern on his face. "Well, it would be your word against mine. Who do you think they are going to believe? Me or a lying struggling actor who is only talented enough to make it on a reality show." He said with a sly grin. I smiled and pulled out an 11x12 envelope from my messenger bag. "What's this?" He opened it with a confused look on his face only to discover that it contained photos I took of us in bed. He took his sunglasses off and looked me in the eyes. He knew I was in control. "Those will be leaked to TMZ and every media outlet if I don't get what I want. Your choice, I can disappear, or we can both go viral." "Okay, done. I want you out of my life for good and you will need to sign an NDA," Jake said. "Not a problem. I get the money in my account and you'll get a signed NDA." "Now that you are getting what you want, I'm assuming you are going to quit." "Not quite yet. I have some unfinished business at Imperial but nothing to concern you because you will soon no longer have ties to the company. I want to stick around for Rachael's demise. It's not just about the money. This is a game that I will see through till the end." "You're a sick fuck." "No, I'm savvy and underestimated." "I don't give a shit. I just want you out of my life. With Mike gone, the company has lost its edge. We are down this quarter and I don't foresee us being up the next quarter with a release not due out until October." "Jake, this isn't a board meeting. Will you have the money wired to me?" "Give me a few days, it will be done. I never want to see or hear from you ever again." "Don't worry Jake, you won't, but we'll always have that one night."

CHAPTER 25

THE MILLIONAIRE
BOYS CLUB

I continued showing up to work the next two days as if nothing was different. I assisted Rachael and did the tasks she'd ask me to do. So far nothing was too out of control, so I was managing fine. That or it's much different working when you know you don't have to. The day after I met with Jake, I received a confirmation of the money being wired to me and I signed the NDA. Stephanie hadn't been seen or heard from in weeks. Rachael sent me out on an errand to grab her lunch, so I decided to take a detour to her condo since I had spare keys. When I arrived at the apartment, I went upstairs to the bedroom and entered the walk-in closet which was half filled with Rachael's clothes and the other half with Stephanie's. They had been shacked up and no one knew, including me. She decided to move in with Rachael after Mrs. Chapman asked her to leave Mike's house. I searched the closet to see if Rachael had the gun that was used to kill Mike. I found the gun along with the silencer in a PS4 box that Rachael had on top of one of the shelves. Rachael didn't strike me as the kind of person that would keep a gun in a safe because she was so messy.

A moment later, I heard the main door slam. I placed the gun back in the box. I heard footsteps and I knew they were Stephanie's. "Shit," I whispered. I was trapped, and I had no idea how I was going to get out. I heard Stephanie coming up the stairs. I went into the walk-in closet again where Rachael kept a disaster of piled clothes. I hid behind several racks of clothes. Stephanie went into the bathroom and she turned on the shower. I heard noises that I didn't think could come from a woman. "Fuck, that hurt." Her ass exploded while she was on the toilet. Thankfully, she was done quickly. I heard the toilet flush and she jumped in the shower. I knew this would be my opportunity to get out. I stepped out of the closet. "Stephanie!" Rachael shouted. *Fuck, I can't catch a break.* Rachael walked into the bathroom. She wouldn't have if she knew what had erupted five minutes earlier. "How are you feeling today?" "I'm good." "What did the doctor say?" "It's a boy." "Sure, why not?" "Another Chapman boy." Rachael appeared to be indifferent and in thought as she sat down on a bench near the shower. She was taking it all in and coming to the realization that she was in a relationship with her dead brother's fiancé who is pregnant with her nephew. She could eventually take the role of stepmother. "Keep it a secret. I'm not going to tell anyone." "Ok, no worries and don't tell any of your model friends. Let's keep this between us." "Yes, I know. Get in here already." I looked through the closet door to see if I had an opportunity to escape. I saw Rachael take her clothes off. I remained in the closet until I heard moaning from the shower. I slowly made my way out, through the bedroom and down the stairs.

I walked back to the office and stopped at the bank to withdraw some cash. When I entered my pin and waited for my account to pull up on the screen. My eyes froze. I had to shut them and open them again. I couldn't believe it but at the same time wanted to make sure it was real. There it was fifty million dollars. I was officially a millionaire, a multi-millionaire. I felt my breath leave my body and then I regained it again. I instantly felt free. Free to do whatever the fuck I wanted. I was never the type to spend money on frivolous material possessions. I had a taste for real estate so immediately my mind was on my home in the hills. I was fantasizing at the moment, but all this had to wait. For now, I had to pretend that my life hadn't changed and none of this happened. I arrived at the office ten minutes later, followed by Rachael shortly after. She arrived in a chipper mood. That would soon change. Rachael received a call from Jake who asked her to come upstairs to the Tower office. Rachael went upstairs oblivious that she was about to be ambushed. Jake had set up a board meeting in the conference room. She walked into the stark conference room at the opposite end of the office. Jake had an entire floor that encompassed his office, a conference room, his personal yoga studio, and a private spa. Yet, he spent the majority of his time in New York, he rarely used any of the spaces. The zen environment was in contrast to the way he and the company did business. Rachael walked into the glass enclosed conference room and was confused to see the twenty board members seated at the table. "Rachael, please have a seat," Jake said. "Hello all, what is this about?" "Rachael, we had been receiving several offers to sell the company. None of them were enticing except the one we received from Adrenaline Games. We were flattered for years by all the interest but scoffed at the idea of selling especially with the revenue that Mike was generating." "We are still generating revenue; I am working my ass off and am generating a shit load of cash so all of your wives could be pumped up with Botox." Rachael interrupted.

"Well, Rachael, we have decided to accept Adrenaline Game's offer this time around. With Mike gone, we don't believe Imperial has the edge anymore. We lost many of the

original team members. It's not the same company anymore."
"Are you fucking kidding me? You have the nerve to call me up here and tell me that you don't think I have what it takes to bring in the numbers that my brother did. You fucking assholes! You are rich because of us!" "We are rich because of Mike," a board member chimed in. "Fuck off, I was running everything when he was in prison! How dare you? You piece of shit. I'm not going to have a dickhead from Adrenaline coming in here telling me what to fucking do or what vision to have. They fucking make sports games. What the fuck do they know about what we do?" "You mean what Mike did. Imperial's success is because of your brother, not you." Another board member said. "Fuck you as you are living in your posh home with your wife and paying for whores on the side. Happily fucking ever after." Rachael stood up. "Jake, you are spineless bastard and all of you think I'm nothing like my brother, huh? Just wait and see. I understand what's happening here. It's because I'm a woman. A woman who is repulsed by the idea of sucking any of your cocks and wouldn't. You can all suck mine." When she returned downstairs, she was on a rampage. She stormed into the office in typical "Mike" fashion and shattered the office door. "This place is fucking bullshit!" I stood up from my desk. "Is everything alright?" I asked. "No, everything is not alright, the fucking assholes upstairs are selling the company." "Well, maybe it's not such a bad thing." "Go fuck yourself, Joaquin, and shut the fuck up. I didn't ask you to speak so don't." "Ok, well, one more thing poor man's K.D. Lang, I quit." "Go, get the fuck out of here!" I grabbed my phone and walked out calmly.

When I made it out to the street, I decided to make a call. "Joaquin, how are you dear?" "I'm fine thanks Mrs. Chapman. Today was my last day at the company, but I wanted to give you a call because I'm concerned about Rachael. She is really losing her mind. Not to mention, I know it's not my place… No, I shouldn't." "If there is something you want to tell me, please do." "It's my understanding that Rachael and Stephanie are living together and have been involved even when Stephanie was with Mike and Stephanie is pregnant." Her tone quickly changed to the cold woman I knew she could be. "Yes, I became aware that she was pregnant at the funeral service. How did you find out?" "I overheard them speaking. I couldn't believe that they could do this to Mike because he was such a great guy." "Joaquin, thank you for telling me. You did the right thing." She hung up. I smiled and felt that Rachael didn't have to worry about Tower or Adrenaline Games. She had to worry about her mother.

I returned to my apartment and couldn't help but think how tired I was of living in the tiny space, and I knew I would definitely make a change, especially since Regan was now with me. Since I was no longer an employee of Imperial and didn't even have to work anymore, I could finally just focus on my acting and finding a home. I sat down to relax and grabbed my laptop. Quickly headlines were surfacing on every gaming blog, more importantly on Kotaku, the gaming blog of all blogs, which meant everyone knew. "Jake Taylor Sells Tower Studios for Five Billion Dollars." The article went on to say how Adrenaline would take control of Imperial Games and guide them into the next era of gaming. It was official, Rachael had lost control. Her short reign as queen of Imperial was over. There was another mass exodus. Both voluntarily and involuntarily. New faces became the norm. The company culture began to change, it became very corporate. The dysfunctional family was gone. Rachael became reclusive with Stephanie and rarely left her home. She was devastated and depressed. Stephanie was four months pregnant and constantly nauseous. Adrenaline immediately took control and advised Rachael to either show up or be replaced. Being a Chapman no longer meant anything. She was trying to create a plan to start a new company, a new empire that would be created by her and no sibling could take credit for it. "Honey, don't worry, everything is going to be fine and work itself out." Stephanie attempted to be supportive.

The doorbell rang and the peephole was blacked out. "Who is it for fuck's sake?" Stephanie repeated. She opened the door out of frustration since there was no response. "Is that the way your mother taught you to speak? I can't say that I'm surprised, dear. And what are you doing in Rachael's home?" Stephanie was speechless and had no idea what to say. "Oh my God, I think my water is going to break." "That's not the only thing that's going to break," Mrs. Chapman said. "Where is Rachael?" "She is upstairs." Mrs. Chapman walked up the stairs dressed head to toe in a black Valentino suit. She opened the door to Rachael's bedroom. "Hello, Rachael." The room was completely dark and the curtains were closed. "Mom!" She sprung out of bed. "Well dear, I see your brother dies and you allow the pregnant cow to move in with you." Mrs. Chapman opened the curtains to brighten the room. "Mom, she's not a cow." "You're right dear, she's also a tramp." "Mom, stop it." Rachael remained at the foot of the bed wrapped in his duvet while Mrs. Chapman stood in front of her with her arms crossed. "Tell me dear, why did you get involved with Stephanie?" "I love her, Mom." "Sweetheart, you don't love her. She was just a way to get back at your brother. Dear, I bore you and I know when you are lying to me and how dare you lie to me for that gold digging social climber." "Mom—enough!" Rachael stood up and walked to the bathroom as Mrs. Chapman followed. She began rinsing her face. "Don't defend her! Mike is barely in the grave and she quickly looked to you for comfort when I threw her out of his house. Clearly this was going on before Mike's death. How could you do that to your own brother?" She emerged from her towel wishing she could wipe away her frustrations. "You always defended Mike; he was always your favorite. He treated me like a fucking peasant, and you always sided with him." "Peasant, dear, if he hadn't given you a job, you wouldn't have the lifestyle you have. You have your brother to thank for all that you have." "No, I have myself to thank. I worked hard for the company." "Enough, take responsibility for what you have done." Stephanie was standing near the bedroom door, eavesdropping. "Mom, I lost it all. They sold the company and I have no control." "Sweetheart, control is something you never had. You were always out of control. Your father, Mike, and I have always had to clean up after you." "Mom, I love her." "I'm done being kind with you, Rachael. It's time for tough love. You either get rid of that puffy monster or you will be disowned from this family. That is not a threat, it's a promise." Mrs. Chapman started to run the bath. "Take a bath, it will do you some good." "Fine." Rachael moped as Mrs. Chapman closed the door. "I'm definitely not ready to be a grandmother," Mrs. Chapman said under her breath.

Stephanie attempted to sneak off away from the door. "Dear, I know you are standing there." Mrs. Chapman opened the door and walked out to the hall. "You will never be a Chapman. The Imperial empire died with Mike; you will never see any of that money. You may be carrying Mike's child, but you will not benefit from this family." "You are such an evil woman." Stephanie said. "What you see as evil is the truth staring at you in the face. You don't care about love or that baby you are carrying. You care about money. I will save you from your misery." Mrs. Chapman pushed Stephanie down the stairs. Stephanie screamed and landed unconscious on the level below. "Rachael, Rachael, hurry dear. Poor Stephanie fell down the stairs." Rachael jumped out of the bathtub and ran out of the room in a towel. "What happened?" "She fainted and fell down the stairs. Call an ambulance." Rachael ran to her phone and dialed 911.

The ambulance arrived and Rachael went with Stephanie as Mrs. Chapman followed in Rachael's car. When they arrived at Cedars-Sinai, she was taken into the emergency room as Rachael and Mrs. Chapman waited in the waiting room. Mrs. Chapman grabbed her mobile phone out of her Prada handbag to make a call. "Hello, dear, we are at the hospital. Such an unfortunate accident. Stephanie fell down the stairs at Rachael's home." "Why was she at Rachael's home?" "I'll tell you later and will update you on how things go here. Goodbye, dear." "Your father sends his love and support," Mrs. Chapman said to Rachael. The doctor emerged from the examination room to speak to Rachael and Mrs. Chapman. "Hello, Ms. Chapman, Mrs. Chapman. We have reached out to Stephanie's mother. It turns out she is vacationing in the Maldives and is on her way here. Stephanie is stable and will be fine. She doesn't remember a thing. Unfortunately, the baby didn't survive. I'm really sorry about this." "Can we see her now?" Mrs. Chapman asked. "Yes, absolutely." Rachael was stunned and sat down. "I'm so sorry, Rachael. Why don't you take a walk? This is a lot for you to deal with. I will check on Stephanie." Mrs. Chapman walked into the room. Stephanie was half asleep. "Wake up, dear." Stephanie opened her eyes and began to cry. "I lost my son." "I know, dear. You fainted by the stairs. I tried to help you, but you slipped from my hands. Your mother is on her way here. I think it's best that you move on from Rachael. If you stay with her, you will have so much grief and will always be reminded of this loss. It's for the best." "I understand." Stephanie wiped her tears off her cheek. Rachael entered the room as Mrs. Chapman exited. "She is feeling better, dear, and is going to be fine. All will be fine." "Thanks Mom." Rachael kissed her mother on the cheek and gave her a hug. She kept her eyes directly on Stephanie as she walked out. "How are you?" "I'm better. I don't remember what happened. I must have slipped down the stairs. I lost my baby." She began crying and attempted to compose herself. "Rachael, I've done some thinking and I think we should go our separate ways." "What? You're not thinking clearly. You've been through a lot. We can start over, start fresh." "I was thinking about this before this happened and now, I just need to walk away." "What? Now that you no longer have Mike's child, you don't want me anymore. My mother was right about you." "No, it's not that. I just think we are better apart, and I don't want to be in Los Angeles any longer. I want to go back to Miami. There is too much drama and baggage for our relationship to survive. Let's end it before we get hurt any further." "This is bullshit!" Rachael stormed out. Stephanie began crying and her mother arrived two days later.

Rachael and her mother stopped in a Starbucks before heading back to her place. They both enjoyed cappuccinos in silence. "You are going to be fine, dear. Everything will work out." "You're right, Mom." "I have to use the ladies' room," she said. As she stepped away, Mrs. Chapman left her phone behind and received a text message. Rachael picked up the phone to read the message.

Hello, Mrs. Chapman. I have been going on a lot of auditions and hopefully one of them will work out. I hope everything worked out with your family. I'm sorry I had to be the one to tell you about Rachael and Stephanie. Hope you are well. Take care. – Joaquin

Rachael was consumed with anger but at the same time placed the phone back on the table and pretended like she hadn't read a thing.

CHAPTER 26

GAME OVER

For the next three months, Rachael was depressed and extremely angry. After she told her mom that she and Stephanie were over, Mrs. Chapman sold Mike's home and returned to Florida. Her work was done. Rachael's was just beginning. She hadn't been to the office and was one week shy of the deadline Adrenaline gave her before they would cut her loose entirely and offer her a package. Rachael decided to go to one of her favorite art galleries to purchase art and photography for her home. It was her guilty pleasure and the only thing that would make her feel better. She was an avid collector of art and photography. She viewed some large-scale photographs, while the gallery assistant walked with her and made suggestions. The owner was away in Palm Springs, so the assistant was looking over things. One particular piece caught Rachael's eye. "We have one of those left. Your former assistant has this piece in his Hollywood Hills home." "What?" "Yes, Joaquin. He loves this photographer and had it delivered last week." "Would you happen to have his address? We didn't have a chance to catch up when he left, I was traveling." "Sure, hold on one second."

Once I left Imperial, I had a month left on my apartment's lease. I decided to break it early and lose my deposit because I could afford to do so. I wasted no time in buying a home in the Hollywood Hills, all within a month. I had been going on several auditions in Hollywood driving my new Mercedes. I was the only out-of-work actor in Los Angeles who had "the home" with a pool and tennis court before "the career." I was also a single parent to Regan. I was getting acclimated to my new life and decided to have lunch with an old friend at the Chateau Marmont who wanted me to meet a casting director friend of hers. She told me he was cute and gay. That was enough for me. I was either going to get cast in something or get laid. Ideally both. The lunch went very well, and the casting director asked me to come see him the next day for an audition. I enthusiastically agreed. Once lunch was over, I headed back home and prepared some lines he had given me. I prepped the whole night by the pool. There was something about reciting my lines under the serenity of the city skyline and the light from my pool. I could hear the crickets chirping and the lines flowed with sheer simplicity, as if they were my own. Afterwards, I went upstairs and into my bedroom. I closed the curtains, took a shower, and jumped into bed, Regan of course jumped in right behind me. I woke-up with the sun beaming on my face. My alarm hadn't gone off yet, but the birds were chirping, and Regan was barking downstairs. "Regan, shut up!" I yelled. I slowly made my way out of bed since I wasn't ready to get up. I looked at the curtains again and figured Lupita must have opened them for me. I hate it when she does that. All of a sudden, as I walked to the bathroom, half asleep, I stopped and realized Lupita was still on vacation and wasn't due back until tomorrow. I looked at the time on my alarm clock and it was shut off. I ran to the bathroom to check the time on my phone because I left it charging on the sink. I felt a huge force against my face, and I plummeted to the floor and I blacked out.

I woke up what I believed was a few hours later with a bloody nose dripping all over my chest. A rope was holding my arms back and I had a noose around my neck. I was on my knees on top of a chair. The rope was attached to one of the exposed beams. All of a sudden, I could feel the rope around my neck tightening and I stood up. I could hear someone behind me as they made their way in front of me. It was Rachael. "How does it feel to have lost, you piece of shit?" "Did I really lose? From my perspective, I won," I said. "How? Both of us will be leaving this house in body bags." "You would have to kill me because no one would believe I committed suicide. The cops may have bought your first ploy at killing Jamal after he killed Mike for you but not this time." "Oh, they will believe it. It's just another tragic Hollywood ending. Wannabe actor kills himself after not being able to land any gigs because he is a self-involved, vain hack with no talent." I began to laugh, "It's better than being someone who always came in second to her brother and would have been nothing without him." "Fuck you." Rachael began punching me in the gut. I began to lose energy and sought refuge in the chair's slight embrace. "By the way, how the hell did you get the money to buy this place? To live this life. Not too long ago you were a fucking assistant. Where did you get the money for all of this?" "I worked overtime, you dumb bitch. That's none of your fucking business." Through my swollen eye, I could see that she pulled out a gun from her jacket. The same gun used to kill her brother. "I never liked you. I don't know why Mike even hired you. I wouldn't have hired you to scrub my floors." I began to laugh under the pain. "Of course not, because you are a fucking pig. You wouldn't be able to get anyone to clean your floors." She hit me with the gun twice in the face. I felt the warm blood drizzling from my head down onto my shoulder. "Is that all you have? You are nothing. Imperial is gone. You are a murderer. You are nothing without Mike except a waste of space."

"Fuck you. Fuck you." Rachael shattered picture frames and lamps. Two of the frames contained images I had purchased it from a gallery. I looked at my bed and my blood was all over my white Frette sheets. "You fucked everything up for me, you worthless piece of shit! Me killing you is actually the easy way out." "Is it? I thought killing your brother was?" I enraged her further and she pounded on my face. "It's so easy to hit me with my hands tied behind me, you bitch." I rocked back and forth in the chair trying to remain on it. She set the gun down on the dresser and pulled out a knife from her pocket. She stood up and stabbed me on the side. "Ahhhhh, you white trash cunt." She began to laugh. "Fuck you." Sunlight streamed into the room as I felt that I would soon "see the light." She turned around and I could tell she was getting into position to kick the chair from under me. Her kickboxing classes were going to come in handy because she was about to kick the chair with brutal force.

She ran towards the chair and I closed my eyes and the last five years began flashing before my eyes at warp speed. All of a sudden, I heard two gunshots go off. I was still standing and wasn't sure if I should open my eyes or not. I opened my eyes and Rachael was on the floor with blood pouring out of her skull. I looked at the doorway and it was Lupita. She was crying. She decided to come back one day early after all and grabbed the gun from the dresser. The gun would not only kill the titan of gaming but also his sibling who always lived in his shadow. "Ay dios mío. Mijo ju okay? Ay dios mío." She dropped the gun and began loosening the rope and helped me down from the chair. She hugged me and called 911. "Jes, I need an ambulance fast. There was a bad woman. Hurry." She hung up the phone and helped me to the floor. I laid down and could hear the ambulance and police sirens arriving. I stared at Rachael's body; her eyes remained open. I slowly closed my eyes and could feel myself being lifted and transported on a gurney. I awoke at Cedars-Sinai Medical

Center with Lupita by my side. I could only see out of one of my eyes because I had a bandage around my head. I wasn't in much pain thanks to the morphine pumping through my system. "¿Cómo te sientes mijo?" "Bien." The nurse came to check on me. "How do you feel?" "Like shit." I smiled. "You are going to be fine. You are very lucky. Your cleaning lady deserves a bonus for saving your life." Lupita smiled, she knew what that meant. "Jes, big bonus." I laughed.

Present Day

A week later, I was back home. I grabbed one of the white towels Lupita had brought out for me. She returned inside the house and continued cleaning the blood in the house that was still left over from the crime. I was told to rest and that's exactly what I did. My arm would remain in a cast for the next four weeks. A month and a half later, I was starting to feel like myself again. I was definitely ready to get back to pursue my acting. Although I didn't get the role, for the audition I missed because of what had happened, another one had come up for a Quentin Tarantino film. My audition was set for the next day. I laid on my sofa preparing for my audition when I heard the doorbell. Regan began barking. *That's strange, how did someone get past the gate?* I grabbed my gun from the credenza just in case and opened the door. When I opened it, there standing with her hair pulled back in a ponytail, skinny jeans and a Chanel jacket was Brenda. "How did you get past the gate?" "J, is that how you say hello to an old friend? Remember, I was an assistant longer than you. A little gate can't keep me out. I heard you need an assistant." "Aren't you getting alimony? Why do you need to work?" "I like to spend money faster than I make it." "Well then, I'm going to need lunch, alkaline water, and take this bitch for a walk. Come back when you have all that done." I handed her Regan's leash and slammed the door.

520 cups of coffee purchased

2,600 calls answered

66,755 emails reviewed

260 lunch runs

1 drug run

260 breakfast runs

36 meetings with repairmen

17 trips to the veterinarian

200 dry cleaning pick-ups

1,350 errands

1,200 dinner reservations

150 personal trainer appointments

3 medical appointments

1 move arranged

1,300 meetings with cleaning lady

25 escorts booked

5 parties planned

3 homicides

1 unplanned adopted dog

1 signed NDA

1 unsigned NDA

GAME OVER